Summer of '82

Coming of Age in the Forgotten South

T. Allen Madding

Charm House Publishing
Thomasville, GA

T. Allen Madding/Charm House Publishing
Thomasville, GA
www.AllenMadding.com
www.charmhouse.pub

Publisher's Note: This is a work of fiction. Names, characters, places, and incidents are a product of the author's imagination. Locales and public names are sometimes used for atmospheric purposes. Any resemblance to actual people, living or dead, or to businesses, companies, events, institutions, or locales is completely coincidental.

Book Layout ©2017 BookDesignTemplates.com
Cover Design ©2021 BookCoverDesign.store

Ordering Information:
This book is distributed by Ingram, One Ingram Blvd., La Vergne, TN 37086. www.ingramcontent.com.

Summer of '82/ Allen Madding. — 1st ed.
Paperback ISBN: 978-0-578-32723-5
Hardback ISBN: 978-0-578-32733-4
Library of Congress Control Number: 2021923339

Dedicated to my brother, Rex Madding.
I have watched you defend your friends and fight for what is
right and just until your eyes were swollen shut and your
knuckles were bleeding. You've never backed down from a bully
or taken the easy way out. You're loyal, trustworthy, and the
kind of friend that always has your back even when the odds are
stacked against you.
Much love and respect.

Allen Madding

Summer of '82

Nothing happens in a vacuum in life: every action has a series of consequences, and sometimes it takes a long time to fully understand the consequences of our actions.
– Khaled Hosseini

Allen Madding

Saturday, June 12, 1982

Allen Madding

{ 1 }

"Buck! Slow the hell down!" Jimmy Lowe shouted as the Chevelle's engine screamed. The rear tires barked as the transmission harshly shifted into second gear. Buck's foot remained firmly planted on the accelerator, which was mashed against the firewall.

"She's the only girl I ever loved!" Buck screamed through tears.

He tossed the car into a turn off the highway. The tires squealed desperately, grasping for traction. Buck counter-steered as the rear of the car slid sideways, momentarily regaining control. He wiped his eyes with the sleeve of his denim shirt, starting the next turn mid-wipe. When he lowered his sleeve, he realized he had missed the entrance of the turn. He jerked the wheel to right the car, but it was too late. The Chevelle struck the curb and vaulted through the air and down into a deep ditch. Huge clumps of dirt and grass exploded in the air as the car hit the earth and bounced back into the air.

Jimmy braced his feet against the floorboard and pressed his hands against the dash. As the car slammed against the ground again, pain shot through Jimmy's legs and hips. The sound of crunching metal dominated the guys' hearing. Finally the car crashed down one last time, rolling onto its roof. The cooler between Jimmy's legs opened, dumping ice and beer cans. Glass shattered and pelted Jimmy's and Buck's faces and hair.

Jimmy tried to make sense of the situation, but the pain in his hips and legs intensified before everything went dark.

Friday, May 28, 1982

Allen Madding

{ 2 }

The summer of 1982 was another hot and dry season in Whitiker County in Southwest Georgia. Ricky Mann rode across his family's farm in his 1972 Chevy pickup with his black lab, Remington, lying beside him on the truck's bench seat. A cloud of red clay dust followed them. The two quietly rode along, monitoring the progress of the center pivot irrigation system, ensuring that the system was moving without hindrance and that water was spraying.

Ricky had spent most of his formative years on the receiving end of bullying at Whitiker County Elementary and more recently at Whitiker County High School. At five foot six, he was a few inches shorter than the rest and seemed an easy target. But as he worked on his family farm, he had developed a firm core, with not an ounce of detectable fat on his 155-pound body. The farm work had also developed what could only be described as his "Popeye" arms, which were usually camouflaged in a work shirt: tight muscular biceps and forearms built from pulling on wrenches and pry bars. As he had grown, Ricky had developed a healthy disdain for bullying, and no one knew that better than the Butts twins, Harry and Carry.

The Butts boys were rough-and-tumble brutes with massive hands that wouldn't fit in a pickle jar. When they weren't bullying classmates, they were wrestling each other. One spring day last year, they decided Ricky was an easy target for their bullying. The troublesome twins elected to corner him on his way to his pickup in the parking lot behind the school. Their miscalculation would be their demise. As Ricky rounded the corner of the school building, he saw the two suddenly dart behind him. Ricky sprinted toward a house at the edge of the parking lot. The twins elected to split up, with Harry following Ricky around the left side of the house and Carry going right to block any escape.

Harry got to the back of the house first, and Ricky slammed his history book across the bridge of the twin's nose. As Harry tumbled to the ground, Ricky swiftly pivoted to meet Carry. Carry swung one of his massive meat-hook fists toward Ricky's head. Ricky ducked the swing and drove one of his cowboy boots into Carry's left knee cap. He heard a loud snapping nose that confirmed that he had struck bone. As Carry slumped forward, grabbing at his knee, Ricky commenced delivering uppercuts to his face with both fists as hard as he could. He slammed the heel of his other cowboy boot into the top of Carry's foot. Carry fell to the ground, spitting blood and snot. Ricky returned his attention to Harry, who was now staggering back to his feet. Ricky grabbed his history book from the ground and jabbed it into Harry's mouth, dislodging a couple front teeth. Before Carry could return to the fray, Coach Peterson rounded the corner.

"Enough!" he shouted.

All three boys turned, shocked to hear the football coach's voice.

"You two picked on the wrong one today!" The coach announced, pointing to the Butts boys. "I've told y'all about picking on the little guy. It caught up to ya today! Now get out of here and leave him alone."

The Butts twins, still spitting blood and teeth, brushed the dirt off their ragged clothes and glared at Ricky. Well, as good as one could glare with suddenly swelling eyes. Without a word, they both turned and started walking in the general direction of their family's rental house.

Ricky dusted himself off and collected his schoolbooks, including his now-soiled history book. He made his way home and turned his attention to his daily chores.

Ricky hadn't spoken of the day's events when his dad walked through the door of the farmhouse at dark, ready for his shower and dinner. As his dad sat down to unlace his work boots, the wall phone rang. He stood up and picked up the receiver.

"Mann Residence," he answered.

"Your kid whipped my boys, and I got a good mind to ride out there and beat your ass!" shouted the voice on the other end of the phone.

Completely unaware of Ricky's dustup, Mr. Mann recognized the voice of Old Man Butts.

"Well, I still got on my old work clothes. Let me tie my boots back up, and I'll go out here and sit down on the porch with my cigar. You just come on out here whenever you're ready. I'll be waiting," Mr. Mann obliged.

He listened as the voice on the other end began to suddenly lose its vigor.

"Well. I don't think...um. Well. I ain't got no problem with you. But my boys both got black eyes. One's missing two teeth, and the other's got a broke nose."

Mr. Mann chuckled. "Two on one and they got their asses skint?"

"Well. Um. Yeah. I guess so," Old Man Butts continued.

"Well. I spec' Ricky taught them a lesson about picking on someone smaller than them and ganging up on a smaller feller. I'd say he contributed to their education. But if you're still sparring for a fight, you come on out. The front gate's unlocked. I'd

be happy to stomp a mud hole in your butt and walk it dry if
that's what you think you need."

"That won't be necessary. But my boys' faces are all torn up."

Mr. Mann laughed louder. "I doubt it hurt their looks any.
Hopefully they learned something from it. Have a good
night...or not."

He hung the receiver up and looked at Ricky. "Guessing the
Butt twins decided to whoop your ass today."

Ricky nodded. "It didn't quite work out like they planned."

"Did you tear your school clothes?" his dad inquired.

" 'Fraid so," Ricky answered.

"Small price for doling out some education. Them two will be
lucky not to wind up in prison."

The Butts twins had indeed learned their lesson, and Ricky
hadn't needed his muscles for much besides farm work since.
The memory still made him smirk a little a year later, and he
replayed the fight as he drove over the farmland. Once Ricky
completed checking the irrigation systems on four fields, he
headed for the three-bedroom ranch house sitting atop a small
rise just past the implement barns. Ricky parked the truck in
front of the house. As he stepped out of the truck, Remington
jumped to his feet and out of the truck. Ricky headed for the

front door while Remington headed for a large pillow under the front porch—a vantage point where he could watch the front yard and driveway. Ricky stomped his boots on the steps of the porch and wiped them on the Astroturf mat before entering the house. When Ricky opened the door of the house, he was greeted with the aroma of fried chicken and turnip greens cooking in the kitchen.

"Get a quick shower. Dinner will be ready in about fifteen minutes," his mother called out to him.

"Alright," Ricky responded. "Sure smells good."

Ricky shed his red-dust-covered blue jeans and T-shirt and stepped into the shower. He turned on the water and let it pour over his head for several minutes before beginning to shampoo the South Georgia soil out of his jet-black hair. After showering and drying off, he pulled on a clean shirt and jeans and headed for the kitchen.

Ricky's father was already seated at the head of the table when he walked into the kitchen. Ricky slid into a chair on the side and poured himself a quart glass jar of iced tea. His mother set a pan of yeast rolls on a hot pad on the table and sat down at the end of the table.

"Ricky, say grace for us," his mother requested.

"Good bread. Good meat. Thank you God. Let's eat," Ricky hastily said.

He lifted his head and reached for the yeast rolls. He tossed a roll onto his plate and passed the pan to his father.

"You ready for graduation?" his father asked.

"Yes, sir," Ricky replied. "Took all my finals today. Got a B average, and I felt decent about the tests today, so I should be good to go."

For the last several months, his classmates had been abuzz about going to college, but Ricky had no college plans. His only plan for future educational pursuits was a welding class at the area technical school. His career plan was to continue working on the family farm like he had since he was fifteen years old. There was a week before graduation ceremonies. The upcoming week would be filled with private parties. Several of his classmates would be headed to Panama City Beach, affectionately referred to as the "Redneck Riviera," following graduation. Ricky had not made any particular plans for post-graduation celebrations.

"You gonna ride into town tonight?" his father asked.

"Prolly so," Ricky answered.

"Alright," his father replied, "try to stay out of trouble and be home before the sun comes up."

Ricky raised one eyebrow.

"No curfew?" he asked.

"Nope," his father answered. "You graduating school and about to turn eighteen. We're gonna trust you with some freedom."

Ricky finished his dinner and carried his plate to the kitchen sink. He walked back to the table and kissed his mother on the cheek.

"Thanks for dinner, Mom," he said. "Delicious as always."

Ricky walked back to his bedroom and retrieved his John Deere ball cap. He tossed it on his head as he crossed the living room headed to the front door.

"Night y'all!" he called over his shoulder as he walked out the front door.

He paused on the front porch, knelt, and rubbed Remington's head.

"I'll be back later," he told the dog. "Keep an eye on things while I'm gone."

He stood, took a glance across the farm, and leapt into the seat of his pickup and headed into town. Haggard, the county seat, was a sleepy little farm town of 3,500 where everything save a couple gas stations, the Dairy Queen, and the Pizza Hut closed up promptly at 5:00 p.m. As he approached town, the Texaco was already closed, but the Flash Foods at the next intersection was open. He pulled in and went inside. The drinking age was eighteen, and although he was a couple months shy, he never seemed to have trouble buying beer. He put a six-pack of longneck-bottled beer on the counter and paid the clerk, who never requested to see his ID. He pulled a bag of ice out of the cooler sitting outside the door of the store. He carefully set the six-pack in the Igloo cooler sitting in the bed of his truck and dumped the ice over the beers.

Ricky eased the truck through the center of town. All the businesses along Main Street were closed, which provided empty parking lots for high school kids to sit and talk. He rounded the corner onto Broad Street and spotted a familiar blue pickup and a red 1970 Chevelle sitting in the city parking lot. The pickup belonged to his hunting and fishing buddy, Jimmy Lowe.

For a high school senior, Jimmy Lowe was an impressive specimen that could be easily mistaken for a full-grown adult with a chest shaped like an oak barrel. At six feet tall and 195 pounds, many wondered why he hadn't played on the football team. His long, straight brown hair, brown eyes, and full beard made for an intimidating figure.

Ricky parked his truck just a few feet from where they were standing and shut the engine off. The red Chevelle belonged to Buck Blue.

Buck had run-of-the-mill features that made it easy for him to blend into a crowd and be overlooked. His sandy blond hair was trimmed in a bowl cut that gave the observer the impression he was the recipient of home haircuts. His steely gray eyes rarely gave hint of his temperament.

In a town as small as Haggard, there were not a lot of choices in activities for teenagers. The American Legion had a huge swimming pool that was open during the summer months. The river was just a few miles away for fishing, and two large lakes were several miles away, offering waterskiing and fishing. Then there was deer hunting, bird hunting, and squirrel hunting. Of course there were high school sports—football, baseball, basketball—and the Legion ran softball teams as well.

There were always some teenagers that had the itch for a little racing. It didn't matter what they drove; they would race their grandmother's Cadillac given the opportunity. To avoid the attention of the local police, they would drive to a two-lane county road just outside of town, line them up, and drag race. Buck held his own with the Chevelle he inherited from his older brother when he turned sixteen. He'd lost once to a kid from out of town that showed up one weekend with a 1972 Camaro. Buck still believed the Camaro had some performance enhancements. His latest defeat had come at the hands of a senior from nearby Revel who had a new Trans Am.

The Chevelle sat shining under the glow of the parking lot lights while a few small beads of water dripped from the bottom of the fenders, hinting of the recent hurried trip through the town's self-serve car wash.

"Y'all raced anyone yet, Jimmy?" Ricky asked.

"No!" Jimmy replied. "I just pulled up here a couple minutes ago myself."

"Y'all made plans for the beach next weekend?" Buck asked, changing the subject.

"I hadn't," Ricky replied. "You?"

"Well, it would seem a waste not to go to the beach. Ya know?" Buck said.

"I'm thinking I'm gonna go," Jimmy chimed in. "I haven't reserved a room or nothing, but I bet we could find a room when we got there. Whadda ya say, Ricky? Will the old man let you away from the farm a few days for a trip to the beach?"

"I reckon," Ricky said. "They both have been hinting at it a bit."

A couple of cars slowly rode by, music blasting through their open windows and their occupants' heads turning to take note of the Chevelle sitting in the parking lot.

"You're getting a lot of attention tonight, Buck," Jimmy noted.

"Yeah, but there's only one gal's attention I want," Buck replied.

For most of the current school year, Buck and Jimmy had both had their sights on the same redhead in their class, Jenny Smith. As the year wore on, the two made their interests known and left Jenny in a position to have to decide on which of the two boys she wanted to date.

Ricky had kept his thoughts to himself, but he was a bit bewildered by the fascination with Jenny. He observed the slowly growing tension between Buck and Jimmy. He hoped that somehow the situation would resolve itself without damaging the friendship that Buck and Jimmy had, but somehow he didn't believe it would. He thought about the intensity of the battles he had witnessed in the woods between two bucks competing over a doe in heat. Many of those battles left one buck with serious injuries and battle scars that it would carry for life if it survived the battle. Ricky wondered what scars his two friends would carry from this for life.

Another group of cars circled through the parking lot, making the loop through town, down to the Dairy Queen, up to the Pizza Hut, and back through the city parking lot. On the second trip through, one of the cars stopped. The driver shut the car off, and out popped a few more of the classmates. Everyone always seemed interested in checking out the Chevelle.

Jimmy reached into the back of his truck and pulled a longneck beer out of a cooler. He slid a flat bottle opener out of his back pocket, opened the beer, and took a long swig off of it.

"Ah," he said after relishing the first cold sip. "Cold beer!"

Ricky grinned. "That sounds like a good idea," he said.

Ricky reached in the back of his truck and retrieved a longneck beer from his cooler. He put the edge of the bottle cap against the back bumper of his truck and hit it with the palm of his hand, and the cap flew off. He saluted Jimmy with his raised beer and took a long sip.

Jimmy retrieved another beer from the back of his truck and tossed it underhanded to Buck. Buck caught it and held out his hand for Jimmy's bottle opener.

"Dang, son!" Jimmy said. "Am I gonna have to get you a bottle opener too?"

"Maybe mount one back by the taillights," Ricky recommended.

Jimmy reached into the cab of his pickup and turned on the radio and pushed in a cassette of Waylon Jennings. He walked to the back of the truck, dropped the tailgate, and sat down. Ricky walked to his truck, dropped the tailgate, and sat down. They both looked at Buck.

"There's one other thing that car doesn't have," Jimmy noted. "A tailgate to sit on!"

Buck ignored the comment and joined Ricky on his tailgate, keeping an eye on the teens admiring his Chevelle. Jimmy had always been opinionated, and his friends knew when to respond and when to ignore.

Jimmy was the instigator among the three. He loved to stir things up and then sit back and watch the drama unfold. He was constantly daring someone to race Buck and constantly daring someone to do something foolish or embarrassing.

After a while, a station wagon pulled into the parking lot. Jenny Smith and two of her girlfriends stepped out of the car and approached the three guys.

"What kind of trouble are the three of y'all stirring up tonight?" Jenny asked playfully.

"We were wondering what it would take to get you to race your mom's station wagon against Buck's Chevelle," Jimmy answered.

"Not happening," Jenny replied with a laugh. "We know what the outcome would be, and I am not about to risk damaging my mom's car, so find another sucker."

"Well, I can't sit here any longer. Wanna go for a ride?" Buck asked her.

"Sure," Jenny replied without hesitation.

The crowd gathered around the Chevelle parted as Buck and Jenny approached. Buck opened the passenger door for her. She walked over and sat down in the car, and he closed the door. Buck hurried around the car, and off they went.

"That won't last long," Jimmy commented.

"Oh?" said Ricky.

"Yeah." Jimmy smiled. "She likes pickup men."

Jimmy and Ricky kept Jenny's friends entertained with conversation and jokes. Ricky had always been amazed at Jimmy's ability to draw an audience and keep them engaged and entertained. Ricky and several other classmates referred to it as Jimmy holding court. He was a natural storyteller, and his life was the material for stories. Often when Jimmy would sit down on a tailgate, one of them would say, "Court is now in session."

Suddenly the Chevelle returned to the parking lot. As soon as it came to a stop, Jenny threw the car door open and scrambled out of her seat and to her feet.

"Don't you EVER do that with me in the car! EVER!" she shrieked, and slammed the car door.

"Girls, we're leaving!" she called over her shoulder as she headed for the station wagon.

Everyone was stunned. The girls scampered to the station wagon, and in a flash they were gone.

"What in the holy hell was that all about?" Jimmy asked.

Buck kept his eyes on the parking-lot asphalt as he walked from the Chevelle back to where Jimmy and Ricky were sitting.

"Red waved us down at the Dairy Queen and wanted me to race his '78 Mustang," Buck explained. "You know I couldn't decline the opportunity to humiliate a Mustang. So we drove out to the Whitiker County Dragstrip"—Buck's nickname for Hardscrabble Road—"and I gave him the butt whipping he wanted. It got a bit sideways on launch, but I drove through it."

"And Jenny lost her mind," Ricky supplied.

"Yeah," Buck said. "She was yelling and waving her hands. I am pretty sure she called me everything but a child of God."

"Oops," Jimmy said.

Ricky noted a bit of sarcasm in Jimmy's delivery. He surmised that Jimmy was continuing to play things cool and collected, allowing his opponent to fail at his own hand.

The cassette in Jimmy's truck came to an end, and an uneasy silence fell among the group.

"Anybody wanna ride?" Ricky asked. "I need to check the irrigation again."

"I'm in," said Jimmy. He walked around to the cab of his truck, shut off the radio, and grabbed a pouch of chewing tobacco from the door pocket. He climbed into the passenger side of Ricky's pickup.

Ricky started the truck and pulled it into gear.

"Guess Romeo struck out this evening, huh?" Ricky observed.

Jimmy chuckled. "Guess so."

They chatted as they drove north of town to Ricky's family's farm. They turned off the highway onto the dirt road through the fields. Jimmy could hear the song of the diesel water pump feeding one of the irrigation systems. Ricky drove up near the pump, shut the truck off, and climbed out. He pulled a flashlight from the dash of the truck and checked the gauges, oil level, and fuel level. He shut off the flashlight and walked back to the truck.

"All good," he said, getting back into the truck.

He drove to the next system. As they drove, their path took them across an earthen dike in the middle of a wet area. The dike had been built to allow the irrigation system to walk across the wet area without becoming mired in the mud.

"Hold up!" Jimmy called. "I'm hearing croakers. Can I use your .22?"

"Sure!" Ricky answered. "Let me grab my spotlight."

Ricky stopped the truck, pulled a spotlight from under the seat, and plugged it into the cigarette lighter in the dash while Jimmy took Ricky's .22 rifle from the rack in the back window. Ricky eased the truck along the dike, shining the spotlight down the banks of the wet area and pausing when he located a set of eyes. Jimmy shot and killed the bullfrogs the spotlight revealed. Ricky stopped the truck as Jimmy hopped out and gathered the frogs.

"Man, we're gonna have a good mess of frog legs right here!" Jimmy said.

Within minutes there was a pile of frogs in the back of the truck. They continued on to the next irrigation system, where

Ricky continued his process of monitoring the pumps. One needed a quart of oil. Another needed refueling. Once they had checked all the systems, they headed back into town.

Arriving back at the city parking lot, they found the rest of the teenagers gone, including Buck and his Chevelle. Ricky pulled alongside Jimmy's pickup and shut the truck off.

"Let's load these frogs on your truck," Ricky said. "I'm sure your folks would love a good frog-leg dinner."

"You sure?" Jimmy asked.

"Yeah, bud," Ricky replied. "I keep the freezer full at our house as it is. Hope y'all enjoy them."

"Thanks!" Jimmy replied.

Once all the frogs were loaded on Jimmy's truck, he headed to his family's house to skin and clean the spoils of his hunt and to get the meat refrigerated.

Ricky put his pickup into drive and headed home.

Allen Madding

{ 3 }

Jimmy drove the handful of blocks from the city parking lot to his parent's home on the south side of town and finished a cold beer on the way. He pulled his pickup into the yard and hurriedly shut it off to avoid disturbing his parents, who he was certain were asleep.

He retrieved the frogs from his truck and took them to a picnic table under a large oak tree in the yard. A light mounted on the back of the house illuminated the picnic table with an orangish glow. He pulled a lock-blade knife from the holster hanging on his belt and methodically skinned out the frog legs. He made quick work of it with skill and dexterity gained from years of cleaning fish and small game. After cleaning them all, he discarded the undesirable parts of the carcasses into a nearby five-gallon bucket and walked into the house. He made a straight path into the kitchen and retrieved a large stainless-steel bowl from one of the kitchen cabinets. He walked back out of the house, stopping at his pickup to retrieve another beer. He slid the bottle opener from his back pocket and popped the cap off the bottle and took a long sip. He walked back to the picnic table and placed all of the frog legs into the bowl. He walked to the side of the house, where a kitchen sink had been plumbed for cleaning fish, and washed the legs. Once he was satisfied they were sufficiently clean, he returned to the kitchen and tucked the bowl into the refrigerator. He took pride in providing food for the family from hunting and fishing and knew his parents would be pleasantly surprised to discover enough frog legs to feed the four of them for dinner.

He washed his hands in the kitchen sink and dried them on the legs of his jeans. He finished off the beer and tossed the bottle in the kitchen trash can before heading to his room down the hall. He sat down on the edge of his bed and pulled off his boots and tucked them under the foot of the bed. He pulled off his socks and threw them at the hamper in the corner. He pulled off his snap-front shirt and his blue jeans and tossed them in the corner. He pulled a T-shirt out of a dresser drawer and pulled it over his head. Finally, he crawled into bed and pulled the sheet over himself. Within minutes, he was sound asleep.

{ 4 }

Ricky woke on Saturday morning to the smell of coffee and fried sausage. He pulled on a pair of shorts and a T-shirt and headed to the kitchen.

"Just in time!" his mother, a petite and dainty woman, said upon seeing him round the corner, peering above a pair of glasses slid down her nose. "I've got sausage, biscuits, and gravy."

"Smells good!" Ricky said, pouring a mug of coffee.

He sat down at the table as his father walked in the front door.

"Do I smell sausage gravy?" his father asked.

"Yes," Ricky's mother answered. "You guys come fix your plates."

Ricky's father walked straight to the kitchen and pulled a plate from a kitchen cabinet. He picked up two biscuits, split them into halves, and covered them in sausage gravy that crept to the edges of the plate. He carried the plate to the head of the table and gently set it down. Ricky followed, making an almost identical plate. While Ricky's father poured a mug of coffee, his mother fixed herself a plate and set down at the table directly across from his father's seat.

Once his father sat down to the table, he removed a worn and dirty John Deere ball cap and started to pray. "Thank you, Father, for biscuits, deer sausage, and gravy. Bless it to our nourishment and us to your hands. Bless our crops and send us some rain. Amen."

"Amen," Ricky and his mother echoed.

For a few minutes, the silence was only broken by the sound of forks against plates. Finally, Ricky's father spoke.

"Ricky," he said. "You look lost in your thoughts. Something heavy on your mind?"

Ricky looked up from his plate and met his father's eyes. "It just seems to me like Jenny is driving a wedge in Buck and Jimmy's friendship. I don't know if the two of them even realize it. And you know Jimmy, he's playing it off like nothing bothers him, but I can almost say for certain that I know it is. Buck on the other hand, he's always been more for being an open book. It's readily obvious that he's getting frustrated with it all. And every time he tries to impress her, it seems to go sideways for him. I just don't want to see them lose a good friendship over a girl. Heck, I don't even understand what all the fuss is all about. She's nice and all, but it's not like she's ever made the homecoming court or anything. I haven't said anything to any of the three of them, because I don't feel like it's my place, but I just get a bad feeling watching all this from the sidelines."

"Yeah. I can understand your wanting to stay out of the middle of it, or you could lose two friends yourself if they thought you were taking sides. Maybe you should take a little time to clear your head from it all. What are your plans today, son?" he asked, looking up at Ricky.

Ricky finished chewing a portion of biscuit, swallowed hard, and said, "I was thinking I might ramble down to the river and see if there were any fish biting. If there wasn't anything needing done around here today."

Ricky's father took a sip of coffee and nodded. "I rode the pivots this morning and everything's running. I don't see why you can't take off whenever you're ready."

Ricky got up from the table, pulled another biscuit from the pan sitting on top of the stove, and returned to his seat at the table. He used the biscuit to mop up the remaining gravy on his plate and finished off the biscuit. He finished off the mug of coffee, stood, and carried the plate and mug to the kitchen sink. He rinsed them both and set them in the sink.

He walked back to his room, pulled on a pair of white tube socks, and laced up a pair of work boots. He walked into the bathroom, ran a brush through his hair, and brushed his teeth. He donned some Old Spice deodorant, and walked out.

As he headed out the front door of the house, his mother called, "Be careful out there!"

"Yes, ma'am," Ricky called over his shoulder as he closed the door.

Remington shook his ears and leaped up from his bed on the front porch and scampered to greet Ricky.

"Come on, boy," Ricky said. "Let's go get the boat ready."

Ricky dropped the tailgate on his pickup, and Remington took the cue to jump up into the bed of the truck. Ricky drove to the implement shed a hundred yards away and backed up to the boat trailer, stopping just inches from the trailer's tongue. He shut the truck off and stepped out of the cab. Remington hopped off the tailgate and scurried to his side.

Ricky loaded his fishing poles and tackle in the boat, and connected the trailer to the truck. He gave the boat one final inspection before patting the truck's tailgate, signaling Remington to leap up.

Once he'd closed the tailgate, Ricky slid back into the cab and started the truck. He grabbed a foil pouch of Red Man chewing tobacco from the dash and put a golf-ball-sized wad in his cheek. As they drove down the dirt driveway to the front gate, he pushed an Alabama cassette in the player and rolled down the window.

Ricky and Remington soon were rolling down the highway into Haggard. Once in town, Ricky turned in to the Piggly Wiggly parking lot. He parked the truck and trailer at the edge of the parking lot across four parking spots. He shut the truck off and eased out of the cab. He paused to rub Remington's head.

"Sit tight for a minute, buddy," he said. "I'll be back in a couple minutes."

It actually took a little longer than that to pick up the chicken-liver bait for the catfish and the bologna, white bread, and mustard for lunch—but only because Miss Jerry at the register was chatty. Within three minutes, he was back to pat Remington's head and fire up the truck. He drove to the corner gas station. He parked in front of the gas pumps, filled the two tanks in the boat and the tank on his truck.

Ricky walked into the gas station, pulled a six-pack of beer from the cooler, and carried it to the counter. Again, the clerk didn't ask him for his ID. He simply rang up the gas and the beer.

"Anything else?" the clerk asked.

"Yeah," Ricky answered. "Give me two bags of ice too."

The clerk rang up the total, and Ricky paid him. He carried the beer out to the truck and set them in the cooler. He grabbed two bags of ice from the ice machine by the store's front doors and filled the cooler.

"Well Remington, let's see who's up for fishing," he as he rubbed between the dog's ears.

Ricky jumped into the cab of the pickup and started driving toward Jimmy's house. As he approached Jimmy's neighborhood, the yards got progressively smaller and less maintained. Several houses nearby had yards of bare dirt. The houses seemed too crammed together for Ricky's taste. He understood why Jimmy liked being in the woods or on the river so much to gain more space.

When he pulled in front of Jimmy's house, Ricky saw Jimmy sitting on an old church pew, playing an acoustic guitar.

"Hey, Johnny Cash," Ricky said. "Wanna go to the river?"

"Does a bear crap in the woods?" Jimmy responded with a grin.

Ricky laughed.

"Give me a minute," Jimmy said as he rose to his feet. He disappeared into the house for several minutes.

"Mom, I'm going to the river with Ricky!" Jimmy called out as he emerged from the house, stowed his tackle box and fishing poles in the johnboat, and piled into the passenger side of the pickup's cab.

Ricky pulled the truck into gear and navigated the streets of town toward County Line Road.

"Thought we'd put in at the county line and go upriver and see what we can find," Ricky suggested. "We can troll downstream with the current when we decide we're as far up as we wanna go."

"Sounds like a fair plan," Jimmy said, poking a wad of Red Man chewing tobacco into his cheek. "Remington ought to be able to sniff out those big catfish for us."

Ricky laughed.

After several minutes of driving, Ricky turned on River Trace Road, which led to the boat ramp. There were a couple pickups with empty boat trailers parked beside the roadway, but no one around. Ricky arced the truck and trailer around and lined the trailer up with the boat ramp. He put the truck into park and got out to prepare the boat for launching. He loosened the web strap across the back of the boat, disconnected it from the trailer, and tossed it into the bed of the truck.

"Alright, Jimmy," Ricky said, "crawl in the boat, and I'll put ya in the water."

Jimmy stepped up on the edge of the boat trailer and hoisted himself over the gunwale of the johnboat. He sat down at the back of the boat near the outboard as Ricky backed into the water. Ricky put the truck into park, stepped out, and released the winch line that was still holding the boat on the trailer.

After tugging the rope on the outboard and giving the engine a little throttle, Jimmy got the outboard to sputter to life, and he eased the boat away from the trailer and out into the river.

Ricky jumped into the pickup and pulled it to the shoulder of the roadway, rolled up the windows, and locked the cab. He lowered the tailgate and looked at Remington, who still patiently stood in the truck bed as his tail wagged wildly.

"Come on buddy," Ricky said.

Remington leaped from the tailgate into the grass of the shoulder of the roadway and to Ricky's side. The two ambled to the water's edge as Jimmy eased the boat toward them.

"Come on, boy!" Jimmy called to Remington.

The dog leaped into the boat and set down between the front and rear seats as if it were his second home. Ricky carefully stepped over the bow of the boat, using one foot to push the boat away from the shore as he did. He sat down on the front seat and pulled on his fishing jacket. Jimmy pulled on the other fishing jacket, leaving it unzipped. He navigated out into the river. The two set quietly watching for snags and soaking in the lush landscape on both sides of the river as they motored upstream.

Both Jimmy and Ricky had spent time navigating the river since they were small children fishing with their fathers. When droughts occurred, it could get so shallow in places that the boat wouldn't float. But when Georgia Power opened the gates on the dam, it could suddenly rise and develop a strong current.

Ricky spoke up. "One of the first times I took this boat out by myself, I went downstream a couple miles from the boat ramp. Just before dark, I started back for the ramp. They had opened the gates on the dam and the current was getting strong. I started doubting this lil nine-horse Johnson was strong enough to overcome the current. For a moment I started getting afraid I wasn't gonna make it back."

"What did you do?" Jimmy asked.

"I looked over at the shoreline." Ricky nodded at a crooked tree by the creek inlet. "I picked out a tree and stared at it. After a little bit, I could tell we were making forward progress. But if you ever took your eyes off the shore and started staring at the current, you would get scared out of your mind."

"I bet that did scare the crap out of you," Jimmy remarked. "Out with your dad's boat on your own for the first time."

"Yeah!" Ricky replied. "You better believe it. The ol' river earned a lot of respect from me that day."

Jimmy continued to guide the boat around the twists and turns of the river as it meandered north. He navigated toward the center of the river, watching for the sandbars and snags that he had almost memorized over the last several years. A crow called out from a tree off in the distance. The shore was lined with cypress trees at the edge of the water and grand oak and slash pine trees further up the bank.

After several minutes of riding, they approached Horseshoe Bend. Jimmy eased off the throttle, slowing to avoid being surprised by oncoming boats as he maneuvered through the bend. Near a deep blue spring, he reduced their speed and steered toward a shady spot on the side of the river. Ricky tossed out a mushroom anchor, fed rope until it found bottom, and cinched it off on a cleat on the bow of the boat.

Ricky removed one of his poles from the rod holders in the side of the boat. He pulled the plastic container of chicken livers out of the cooler, pulled a large liver out, and ran a hook through it several times. He handed the container of chicken livers to Jimmy, who had already gotten his fishing pole in hand. Ricky cast the hook and bait a short ways toward the bank and took his thumb off the thumb stop on his Zebco 33 spinning reel. He let it fall into the dark, murky water. After judging it was at the depth he wanted, he twisted the crank lever until he heard the familiar clunk.

In the back of the boat, Jimmy had performed almost the identical maneuver. Ricky rested the pole against the side of the boat and picked up his second rod. He baited it and cast the baited hook another twenty feet or so from the first. When he looked to the back of the boat, Jimmy already had both of his lines in the water and was quietly monitoring them.

"Ready for a cold beer?" Ricky asked.

"Thought you'd never ask!"

Ricky opened the cooler, tossed a beer to Jimmy, and opened one for himself.

A year ago, Jimmy had goaded Ricky into changing beer brands. Ricky was introduced to Michelob when he first started drinking beer just after getting his driver's license.

One night Jimmy looked over at him and said, "You know, a lot of girls drink Michelob. It is good beer. Don't get me wrong, but you need to learn to drink a man's beer."

"And what would that be?" Ricky asked.

Jimmy rubbed his hand through his developing beard and said, "Budweiser!"

Now the two of them sat in the middle of the river, drinking Budweiser to cool off, and Jimmy looked at Ricky.

"You know, Ricky," Jimmy started. "Budweiser is a good beer and everything. Don't get me wrong, but a lot of girls drink Budweiser. You need to learn to drink a man's beer."

Ricky laughed. "And what would that be, Jimmy?"

"Busch!" Jimmy said, holding the "sh" sound long for effect.

"Busch?" Ricky asked, to make sure his ears hadn't deceived him.

"Yeah!" Jimmy said. "It's a man's beer. You won't see many girls at the lake or on the beach drinking Busch."

"Right," Ricky responded. "But is that because they're girls or because it isn't any good?"

Jimmy chuckled. "Maybe both, but a man's gotta drink a man's beer. Busch!" Jimmy repeated the name and again held the "sh" sound a bit longer than usual for effect. "When you pop the top, it says its name!" he pointed out.

"Hey!" Ricky said as one of the poles took a hit.

He grabbed the rod handle and picked it up and gave it a tug. The rod tip bent toward the water and the rod felt heavy in his hands.

"I got one!" Ricky reported as he hurriedly reeled in the line.

The fish tried to turn for the bottom as Ricky pulled up on the fishing rod. He cranked the reel and the rod tip bent back toward the surface of the water. He pulled it up again and once again cranked on the reel. After a few more repeated cycles, Ricky reached over the side of the boat, grabbed a channel catfish below the two side fins, careful to avoid the sharp barb as the fish squirmed on the hook, and pulled it out of the water.

"Maybe about four pounds," he estimated as he removed the hook from the fish's mouth.

He strung the fish on a stringer and secured it to a cleat on the side of the boat, and eased the fish back into the water.

As Ricky re-baited his hook, Jimmy grabbed one of his poles that was bending toward the water. Jimmy commenced fighting the fish. Every time he would stop cranking the reel, the line brake would squeal as the fish pulled line back out. He cranked the reel and pulled against the fish. Suddenly the line broke and he stumbled backwards in the boat before regaining his balance.

"Well, hell!" he exclaimed.

"He get away?" Ricky asked.

"Hell yeah!" Jimmy replied. "I think he went to the bottom and went around an old cypress stump or something."

Ricky shook his head in disbelief. "Or he ran into an old sunken car and rolled up the window."

"You don't really think there are old cars in the bottom of this river. Do you?" Jimmy asked.

"I dunno," Ricky answered. "I've heard stories of folks running 'shine running cars off into the river. But I'd think if that happened, they'd be closer to where the old County Line Bridge is."

"The way he fought, he'd have to have been an eight- or ten-pounder," Jimmy said as disappointment dripped from his face.

Jimmy opened his tackle box, tied a new hook on the line, and placed a sinker weight just above the hook. He baited the hook and made a cast back out in the murky water.

He soon got a hit on his other pole and landed a channel catfish that he guessed was a little over five pounds.

Around midafternoon, they both made themselves bologna sandwiches, still monitoring their lines. Remington quietly eased from one boy to the other, managing to obtain a corner of each of their sandwiches.

Within a few hours, their two stringers held twelve channel catfish that weighed between four and eight pounds each.

"Well, we're out of bait and out of beer," Jimmy reported.

"Guess it's time to head in then," Ricky replied.

They pulled up the heavy stringers and stored their fishing poles in the rod holders on both sides of the boat, and Jimmy started the outboard. He eased the boat forward to the anchor line, relieving the tension on the line. Ricky pulled the anchor into the boat. Jimmy turned the boat down the river and headed for the landing.

"You know, I've been thinking," Jimmy spoke up over the hum of the outboard.

"That can be dangerous!" Ricky responded with a smirk.

"We ought to get some crickets from Wisham's Bait Shack and catch some bream," Jimmy continued.

"OK," Ricky replied slowly, waiting for Jimmy's plan to get more interesting.

"Then," Jimmy continued, "we use the bream as bait fish with a large weight and fish some of these deep holes for the big flat-head catfish. The old folks talk like they get over twenty pounds."

Ricky considered the idea for several minutes before he spoke. "We're gonna need some heavier test line for fish that size, maybe even heavier reels. But we did locate several of those deep holes during the drought last year."

Jimmy grinned as Ricky seemed to be warming to the idea.

"My dad's got a Zebco 808 that he fishes saltwater with from time to time," Jimmy said. "I bet it would handle it."

Ricky gazed out at the river and rubbed Remington's head.

"I can check and see if they have an 808 at Wisham's or at Harrell's Hardware," Ricky said.

When they reached the boat landing, Jimmy eased the boat to the edge of the bank. Ricky and Remington leaped onshore. The boys packed the boat within just a few minutes with practiced efficiency.

Ricky drove to Jimmy's house and parked at the edge of the street. The screen door on the house opened, and out stepped a man with a worn leather face, a dirty Mack truck baseball cap, and a tired scowl that Ricky quickly recognized as Jimmy's father.

"Y'all catch anything?" he asked in a gravelly voice.

Jimmy smiled as he hoisted a stringer from inside the boat.

"We both got six decent-size channel cats," he said.

"Well, your mom is frying up the frog legs for dinner, so get your fish cleaned and in the fridge. Dinner will be ready in a bit," he replied.

Jimmy laid the stringer of fish in the fish-cleaning sink beside the house. He walked back to the boat, retrieved his two poles and tackle box, and set them on the porch.

"Well, I better get moving!" Ricky said. "See you at the OK Corral after dark."

Jimmy chuckled. "Sounds good," he replied, recognizing the reference to the city parking lot.

Ricky eased into the truck, started the engine, and headed back to the family farm.

Allen Madding

{ 5 }

Just after sunset, Buck walked out the back door of his parents' house and across to his Chevelle, parked under a large water oak tree. He had spent the afternoon changing the oil in the car and washing it. He stopped at the front of the car and polished a smudge on the chrome bumper with a rag from his back pocket. He gave the car one final glance before sliding in under the steering wheel and starting the V-8 engine. The engine roared to life with a pleasant note and the low rumble of the dual exhaust. He loved the sound of the engine's dual exhaust so much that he always shut the radio off whenever he raced someone, so he could listen to the throaty song of the exhaust system. As he reached the street in front of the house, he stomped the throttle. The rear tires spun in the dirt driveway, struggling to gain traction as Buck sharply turned the steering wheel. The rear of the car flipped up onto the asphalt street with a loud squeal. The smell of burnt rubber filled the car. His face broke into a grin. He pushed the My Home's in Alabama cassette into the car's stereo and sang along with Alabama as he made the short three-mile drive into town.

When he reached town on Broad Street, he could see the parking lot was empty. He elected to make a loop through town and see who was around. No one was sitting at the Standard gas station, he noted. There were a couple cars sitting at the Bank of Haggard. He hung a right at the highway, jogged down it a half mile, and made a left into the Dairy Queen—no cars caught his eye there, either. He made a loop through the parking lot and headed back north. When he reached the Pizza Hut parking lot, he made a loop around the building. He recognized a few cars from school and a few faces through the windows. He swung the Chevelle back onto the highway. He made a U-turn in the turn lane in front of the Texaco and headed back to the city parking lot.

When he reached the parking lot on Broad Street, he saw Jimmy's truck sitting driver's door to driver's door with Jenny's mother's station wagon. He could see Jimmy and Jenny deep in conversation. He slammed his palms against the rim of the steering wheel in frustration. He turned in to the parking lot, made a loop, and headed back through town again.

On his second lap through town, he saw Ricky coming in from the highway. He flagged him into the driveway of the Bank of Haggard.

"Wassup, Buck?" Ricky asked from his pickup.

"Ain't nothing to it," Buck replied. "Didn't wanna interrupt the lovebirds at the OK Corral. Wanna ride a bit?"

"Sure," Ricky answered. He rolled up the window on his truck, shut off the ignition, and stepped out. He walked over to the passenger side of the Chevelle carrying a red Solo cup he was using for a spit cup while he chewed tobacco. He opened the passenger door and slid into the seat of the Chevelle.

Buck eased back out onto Main Street and continued on another loop through town. As they approached the Flash Foods at the corner of the highway, Ricky pointed out a new white Mustang. "Oh yeah," he said. "Andy Mathis has got a new 5.0 Mustang. Reckon he's feeling his oats?"

Buck chuckled and turned in to the gas station as Andy was walking out of the store and heading back to his car.

"Hey, Andy!" Buck called out.

"Hey, Buck," Andy responded.

"I see ya got you a new car," Buck said.

"Yeah, folks bought it for me this week as a graduation present," Andy explained.

"Nice!" Buck responded. "Just in time to take to the beach after graduation."

Andy grinned. "That's my plan. I've been saving all my money from my job at the Haggard Builders Supply for the beach."

Buck nodded his head. "Should we see what it'll do?" he asked.

Andy thought for a second, then replied with a grin, "Yeah. I'm game."

Andy crawled in the car, started the engine, and pulled away from the gas pumps to the edge of the highway. When the traffic was clear, he pulled out and headed south with Buck following close behind in the Chevelle. Just south of town near the Magnolia Motor Court, he turned left and then made a right on Hardscrabble Road—the Whitiker County Drag Strip. The road had been carefully selected for its remote location, which was rarely patrolled by the county sheriff's only two cars, for the sparsely located houses, and for the road's long straightaway providing a quarter mile and a cool-down stretch. They drove a couple miles out to where there was a faded white line spray-painted across the roadway.

Andy pulled to the line in the right lane while Buck pulled alongside in the left. Ricky held up one finger, counting aloud and on his hand at the same time. "One, two, three!" he shouted.

Andy and Buck floored the throttle in both cars at the same time. The Chevelle spun the tires and wiggled before gaining traction. The Mustang gave a light chirp of the tires and launched straight, getting a fender out in front of the Chevelle. Buck slammed gears with the chrome Hurst shifter on the Muncie four-speed transmission. Once he'd grabbed second gear, the four-barrel Quadrajet carburetor on the Chevelle bellowed its deep moan. The Chevelle squared up to the Mustang and nosed ahead.

Buck slapped the shifter into third gear, and the Chevelle pulled away from the Mustang as if it were tied to a stump.

Buck laughed. "That brand new 5.0 ain't got nothing for this 350!" he exclaimed.

Buck let off the throttle at the road sign that local racers knew marked a quarter mile from the painted stripe. He lightly pressed on the brake and downshift. Once down to around thirty miles per hour, Buck eased the right-side tires off onto the grassy shoulder of the road. He dropped the transmission into first, punched the throttle, and snatched the steering wheel. The car kicked up a cloud of dirt and grass as the back end spun around 180 degrees and hit the asphalt. The tires squalled as they struggled to grab traction, leaving two black streaks on the rough asphalt and filling the air with the smell of hot rubber. Buck grabbed second gear and eased off the throttle. Andy pulled up driver's door to driver's door, and they both stopped in the roadway.

"Guess this thing has a highway gear in it," he said.

"Apparently it ain't got a scat gear!" Ricky called from the passenger side of the Chevelle.

They all three laughed.

"Reckon I owe you a beer," Andy said to Buck.

"To the winner goes the spoils," Buck quoted in answer.

Andy reached down in the Mustang and came back up with a can of Budweiser. He held it out the window to Buck. Buck grabbed it, popped the top, and took a big swig.

"The only thing better than a cold beer is a free beer!" Buck shouted.

Buck eased the clutch out and headed back into town while polishing off his winnings.

When they reached the city limits, Buck drove down Main Street, continuing to the Courthouse square, made a left onto Broad Street, and turned right into the city parking lot. He immediately noted Jenny's station wagon was gone, and Jimmy's pickup was sitting at the second driveway. He drove over to it and parked the Chevelle. Andy pulled up just behind both vehicles and parked the Mustang. When both engines were silenced, the guys could hear Hank Williams Jr. singing "A Country Boy Can Survive" from the radio in Jimmy's truck. Jimmy was sitting on the tailgate of his pickup, holding court with several of their classmates. He was wearing a straw cowboy hat, jeans, a snap-front western shirt, and cowboy boots and drinking a beer from a longneck bottle.

"Is that the latest victim?" Jimmy asked, waving the neck of the beer bottle toward the Mustang.

"Hell, yes!" Buck replied with a grin.

Jimmy smiled. "The old Chevelle's still pretty stout even against new iron."

"Yeah it is," Andy commented from the edge of the semicircle of teenagers gathered at the back of Jimmy's truck. He looked slightly dejected but good for the wear.

"Don't take it too hard, Andy," Jimmy called out to him. "No matter how big and bad you are or how fast your car is, there's always gonna be someone just a little bit bigger, just a little bit badder, and just a little bit faster than you are. It's just how life works. Our football team has learned that over the last four seasons, and the wrestlers on Georgia Championship Wrestling have learned that lately. Look at Rodney Piper. He came out acting all big and bad telling everyone not to call him Rodney no more, that he was changing his name to Roddy. What did Dusty Rhodes say to that? He said, 'Rodney, Rodney, Rodney.'"

Ricky laughed real hard. Andy nodded his head and grinned.

"It's like my old buddy Ricky over there," Jimmy continued. "We were out on his farm last fall, hunting dove. The low ones would fly over and Buck and I would shoot 'em down with our twelve gauges and argue over who shot it. Ricky over there, he brought his granddaddy's sixteen-gauge full choke. Ol' bird would come flying over so high I was sure it had on an oxygen mask. Buck and I didn't even bother making a shot, because we knew he was out of range. Ol' Ricky would stand up from the five-gallon bucket he was sitting on, make one shot—BOOM!—and the bird would spiral down to the ground. No arguments. No questions asked. We all knew who shot that one. Always someone a little bit bigger, a little bit badder, a little bit faster, or a little bit better. It keeps the ego in check so you can get your head through the doorway. Ol' Buck was getting a pretty swole head for a while when he was undefeated for like a whole school year, but even he got knocked down a peg a time or two over the last few months."

Buck kicked the surface of the asphalt parking lot with the toe of his tennis shoe. "It happens," Buck said, still looking down. "Don't have to like it. Just know it happens. Accept it and roll with it." Jimmy's words stung at Buck's pride, but he managed not to let it to show. He suspected Jimmy had intentions of knocking him down a peg with Jenny as well.

Jimmy swallowed off the remainder of his beer and tossed the empty bottle over his shoulder into the bed of his truck. He pulled a folded aluminum pouch from his shirt pocket and stuffed a golf-ball-sized wad of Red Man chewing tobacco into the cheek of his mouth.

"The Red Man reaction," Jimmy said, quoting the TV and radio commercial. "Satisfaction!"

Buck shook his head. "I don't know how you do it," he commented. "I'll stick to Beechnut. Red Man is just too strong!"

"So what's the plan for next week, boys?" Jimmy asked. "Graduation is Saturday, and sounds like over half the class is going to Panama City Beach."

Buck looked up. "I'm going."

Ricky chimed in, "Yeah, I think I am too."

Andy and a few of the others in the small crowd piped it with "I'm going."

Several fractured conversations initiated about who was staying where and who they'd heard was going.

Jimmy looked at Ricky and Buck. "Either of you made any room reservations?" he asked.

Buck replied, "My brother and I got a room reserved at the Trade Winds."

Ricky shook his head. "Nah," he answered. "I figure there ought to be some rooms available somewhere."

Jimmy spat tobacco juice on the asphalt to the side of his truck. "Yeah. There's plenty of motor lodges across from the beach if we can't find something available on the water."

Ricky nodded. "Works for me."

"Ya know," Jimmy said. "The beer down there is cheaper than it is here. I hear you can get some pretty good bargains if you swing by one of the grocery stores."

"Nice!" Ricky said.

One of the two city police cars leisurely cruised through the parking lot. Those who had a beer slid it in their pants pocket or behind them on the hood of the car they were propped against. The police car didn't stop. It just lazily turned onto Broad and headed south. On occasion, someone wouldn't move fast enough to hide their beer, and the city police would give them a stern lecture on drinking in public and underage drinking and make them pour it out. But they never made any arrests for either of the offenses, and everyone standing in the parking lot knew it. Still, since it was a small town, rumors passed the news faster than the biweekly Haggard Enterprise newspaper could. No one wanted one of the cops telling their parents they'd been caught drinking, so they tried to be coy about it. Around 11 p.m., Ricky looked at his watch.

"Well," he said, "I need to go check on the pivots and get to bed."

Buck dropped Ricky off at his truck. As Ricky fired the truck up for the drive home, he unlatched the vent window and pivoted it out to scoop a little of the cool evening breeze into the cab on the way home. As he drove past the city parking lot, he honked the car horn once and threw up his hand in a wave to the teenagers still gathered like an audience at the back of Jimmy's truck. As he drove by, he saw Jimmy throw up a one-finger wave in return.

Allen Madding

{ 6 }

Just after 8 a.m., Ricky woke to a pounding on his bedroom door.

"Get up and get showered and dressed," his dad called out. "Breakfast will be ready in a few."

Ricky knew he didn't have the luxury of sleeping late. It was Sunday, and that meant the weekly drive to the Haggard United Methodist Church. After a shower and minimal preparations, he got dressed and followed the scent of eggs and fried ham to the table.

After breakfast, Ricky's parents headed to church in his father's truck, while he drove separately in his. For years, they had all ridden in one automobile, but now he was allowed to enjoy a sliver of independence. When they reached town and turned down Broad Street, his parents parked on the curb in front of the church. Ricky proceeded around the corner and parked in the lot behind the church alongside some of his classmates' cars and trucks. He headed into the education building through the basement entrance and took the stairs up to the Sunday school assembly room on the second floor. When he walked in the door, he immediately saw Andy, Gil, and Ford chatting near the windows.

"Wassup, guys?" Ricky greeted them.

"Wassup, Ricky?" Gil responded. "Andy was telling us that he got smoked by Buck's Chevelle last night."

Ricky chuckled. "Yeah, his new Mustang put up a good fight, but it wasn't quite strong enough."

Rob Hight, a local attorney and the father of one of the girls in the youth group, soon walked in the doorway.

"What's going on in here?" he asked with a smirk.

A couple of the youth startled at his entrance, but Ricky, Andy, Gil, and Ford had become accustomed to the weekly routine and didn't flinch.

"Morning, Mr. Hight," they responded almost in unison.

Just a few steps behind Mr. Hight walked a slender college-age blonde girl that they recognized as the summer youth director. She had an acoustic guitar hanging across her back.

Gil commented, "I'm glad to see a guitar. That means we can sing something other than the hymns!"

The dozen teenagers gathered in the room chuckled in agreement. After the blonde girl led them in a few songs, they divided into two groups and headed to classrooms.

Ricky, Andy, Gil, and Ford entered their classroom, which had been furnished with a sofa, a love seat, and a couple recliners donated by the boys' families in place of the metal folding chairs in the other rooms. Ricky plopped down in a recliner and threw one leg over the arm. Andy, Gil, and Ford divided between the love seat and sofa, leaving the remaining recliner for Mr. Hight. They chatted among themselves until he walked in and closed the door behind him.

"Y'all got big plans for the summer?" Mr. Hight asked.

Ricky instantly answered. "I'll probably go to the beach after graduation for a few days, and then work on the farm like any other summer."

Andy spoke up. "Yeah, I'm gonna go down to the beach too. Then probably just hang around town, go to the Legion pool and the video game room until time to head to school."

"Where ya going?" Mr. Hight asked.

"Valdosta State College," Andy answered.

"How 'bout you, Gil?" Mr. Hight asked.

"Yeah," Gil said. "My summer sounds like Andy's. Hang out around town till orientation at school."

"Where you planning on going to school?" Mr. Hight asked.

"Georgia Southern College in Statesboro," Gil replied.

"What about you, Ford?" Mr. Hight asked.

"Well," Ford started, "I got a few customers lined up for lawn mowing. I thought I could stash away a little money before school starts up this fall at the University of Georgia—Go Dawgs!"

Mr. Hight didn't start into the pre-planned lesson per the schedule for all United Methodists to study that week. He left that tucked into his weathered extra-large King James Bible. Instead, he provided an impromptu talk on graduation, going out into the world, and the magnitude of decisions.

"Boys, ya'll will probably forget most of the things I have said to you in here over the last couple of years," he said. "But if you remember anything, remember this: Every decision you make in the days and weeks to come can impact the rest of your lives. No matter how small a decision it is, take a minute to consider the consequences of your choices and try to make wise decisions."

He paused and peered over the top of his reading glasses at each one of them, but none of the boys made eye contact.

"Over the next several months," he continued, "you are going to be faced with all kinds of decisions. Don't take any decisions lightly. Remember that a small decision made in haste can have a lifelong impact. When conflicts arise, choose carefully how you respond and consider the impact on friendships and family. If you choose to drink, do so with moderation and don't drink and drive. Try to remember what your mamas and daddys have told ya, don't forget where you came from, and stay close to God. When you're making choices, consider what would honor your family and what would honor God. And lastly, remember no matter what happens, you can always come home."

He closed his comments with a prayer and dismissed the boys. They each quietly stood to their feet and headed out to the hallway and down the front stairs to the front sidewalk. They joked and chatted as they walked up Broad Street to the Standard station on the corner. While the gas station was closed on Sunday, the vending machines were operational. Ricky bought a bottle of Coca-Cola and a package of Tom's Toasted Peanuts. He opened the bottle using the opener in the front of the machine and tore the corner off the pack of peanuts. He stepped away from the machine, took a quick sip of the Coke, and carefully poured the peanuts into the bottle. Several of the other boys did the same. A few only bought a drink, and a couple just walked with them for the company.

Everyone in the group finished their drinks and stowed the empty glass bottles in the rack next to the machines. As they walked back to the church for the main worship service, Ricky could feel a trickle of sweat running down the back of his Sunday shirt. He despised having to wear the dress shirt and tie every week and silently questioned why he couldn't wear jeans and a T-shirt to church. But he didn't want to get a lecture from his mother, so he toed the line for the expected Sunday-best dress code.

They walked down the sidewalk and then up the stairs leading to the three sets of double doors at the front of the sanctuary. The center doors were open. Ricky couldn't remember a time that he ever saw the other two sets of doors opened and wondered if they suited any purpose other than appearance. They walked inside and proceeded down to the second row of pews. The big pipe organ was playing what Ricky referred to as funeral dirges as they entered.

The Methodist church used what they called acolytes—two young children who lit the candles on the altar at the beginning of the service and extinguished them at the end of the service. Ricky had served in the role when he was younger and was very familiar with the process of trimming the wicks on new candles before a service so that they would light properly, as well as the significance and symbolism of walking down the aisle carrying the flame, lighting the candles, and later carrying the flame out after extinguishing the candles. Unfortunately for the two boys serving as acolytes this Sunday, Ricky also remembered how the taper, the long wood and brass device used to light and extinguish candles, was assembled. The acolytes set on the pew just in front of Ricky and his friends. Once they had completed their initial duties of lighting candles, they would slide their tapers under their pew to await the end of the service, when they would be called back into duty. Ricky quietly put one of the toes of his cowboy boots on the brass head of the taper and the other on the wooden handle. He gradually unscrewed the wooden handle of the taper by sliding his foot forward over and over. At almost the same time, Ford was doing the same thing to the other acolyte's taper. As the last verse of the last hymn was being sung, the two acolytes reached under their pew to retrieve their tapers, only to come up with the wooden handles. They both grabbed the remainder of the tapers and hastily reassembled them while casting knowing looks over their shoulders at Ricky and Ford, who returned their glances with huge grins.

When the service concluded, a large crowd headed to the local buffet next to the old firehouse. It was a tradition of sorts with Ricky's family and most of the other churchgoing families in town. Everyone knew they needed to make the block trip rapidly in order to beat the Baptists to the fried chicken. The parking lot quickly filled as a testament to the quality of the food and the scarcity of restaurant choices—the choices were slim on week-days and even slimmer on Sundays.

After a hearty meal of chicken, mashed potatoes, and every veg-etable a Southerner could imagine, Ricky's family headed out. His father stopped beside Ricky's pickup before they left for the farm."

"Got any plans today?" he asked.

Ricky nodded. "A bunch of kids from school are having a senior lake party at Lake Birdsee. I thought I'd ride down there and do a little waterskiing."

"Alright," his father replied. "Try not to get in any trouble."

Ricky grinned. "No, sir!" he responded.

Back at the farm, Ricky changed into a bathing suit and T-shirt. He slapped an old, worn straw cowboy hat on his head as he headed out of his room. He grabbed a beach towel from the hall closet, walked out to the yard, and climbed into his truck and headed back toward town. Georgia laws forbade selling beer on Sundays, but Ricky had picked up an extra six-pack on the way home Saturday night that was still sitting on ice in the cooler in the back of his truck. He stopped at the Flash Foods on the edge of town, purchased another bag of ice, and poured it into the cooler to ensure there would be no warm-beer crisis. Then back into his truck and south to Revel he went.

When he turned in to the driveway in front of the clubhouse at
Lake Birdsee, he recognized several cars and trucks near the
boat ramp. He parked alongside the line of cars and stepped out
of the truck. He carefully scanned the horizon of the lake, recognizing a few boats. A faded yellow sixteen-foot tri-hull boat
with a walk-through windshield pulled up to the edge of the
shore and silently slid up on to the sand.

"Jump in, Ricky!" shouted Jimmy.

Ricky chuckled—he should have known Jimmy would already be
on the water. Ricky heaved his cooler into the boat. He leaned
into the boat, using his legs to push it off the sand back into the
water, then leapt in.Jimmy fired the outboard and took them to
the middle of the lake.

"You ready to ski?" Jimmy asked.

"Sure!" Ricky replied.

He pulled on a fishing life jacket that had four pockets on the
front, grabbed a cold can of beer from the cooler, and jammed it
into one of the life jacket's pockets. After pulling the ski rope
out from under one of the cushions in the front of the boat,
Ricky clipped one end to a ring on the back of the boat, tossed
the handle out into the lake, hurled two skis out as close to the
rope handle as possible, and jumped in the lake. He slid a foot

into the boot on each ski, grabbed the rope handle, and aligned himself with the rear of the boat.

"Alright!" he shouted to Jimmy. "Tighten up the slack."

Jimmy eased the boat forward until the rope was tight.

"GO!" Ricky hollered.

Jimmy jammed the throttle lever forward, and Ricky popped up out of the water seemingly effortlessly. He immediately put the ski rope handle in the crook of his elbow, pulled the can of beer out of the pocket of the fishing jacket, popped the top, and steadily drank the beer as he skied across the lake. As they met or passed other boats, he would raise the beer in salute or pull his cowboy hat off and wave it at the other boaters.

After a few laps around the lake, Ricky had finished his beer. He motioned at the boat ramp. Jimmy recognized the signal and made a turn toward the boat ramp. Just on the other side of the ramp was a small peninsula with a group of bikini-clad girls, Jenny, Mary, Terri, and Carol. He maneuvered within about twenty feet of the peninsula before making a sharp turn back into the center of the lake. Ricky cut his skis to shoot himself outside of the wake toward the shore and tossed the ski rope handle. He laid back a little to the rear of the skis to bring the toe of both skis just above the water. The velocity took him straight to the end of the peninsula. With the toes of the skis raised, when he reach the edge of the shore, the velocity propelled him right up on the land. He popped out of the boots on the skis and ran a bit to break his momentum, stopping standing upright on the shore. All of the girls cheered as if he had completed an event at the Olympics. He tipped his cowboy hat to the crowd and took a bow.

Jimmy circled back with the boat and stopped at the dock. Ricky climbed back in, sliding the skis back over the nose of the boat, and pulled in the ski rope.

"Anyone wanna ski?" Jimmy called to the girls on the shore.

Immediately, the four girls headed for the boat.

"We're in!" shouted Jenny.

"OK, I'm up," Jimmy said. "Ricky, you're driving."

They switched places at the controls of the boat. Ricky dug into the sidewall storage compartment and retrieved a cheap captain's hat that he had purchased at a bait store a few months earlier. He stowed his cowboy hat and donned the captain's hat.

"Welcome to Captain Spiffy Tours!" he exclaimed.

The girls laughed. Ricky backed them away from the dock and into the body of the lake. He maneuvered the boat out into the middle of the lake. Jimmy tossed the handle of the ski rope out into the water behind the boat, allowing it to pull the remainder of the ski rope over the edge as the boat continued moving. He sat down on the transom next to the outboard, drinking a beer. When he finished the beer, he tossed the can onto the floor, and without saying a word, he suddenly leaned backwards and out of the boat.

One of the girls squealed, "Oh my God! Jimmy fell out!"

Ricky laughed. "Yeah no," he said. "Jimmy launched himself out of the boat."

Ricky cut the throttle to neutral, allowing Jimmy to catch the ski rope handle as the rope snaked by him. He tossed the skis out to him. Jimmy pulled the bindings of each ski over his feet, pointed the toes of the skis to the sky, and navigated the ski rope between the two skis.

"Hit it!" he called out.

Ricky slammed the throttle forward, and Jimmy popped up out of the water almost automatically. Ricky eased back the throttle to a comfortable speed for skiing and looked over his shoulder at Jimmy.

Wasting no time, Jimmy reached forward on the ski rope and pulled himself some slack. He placed the handle behind both of his knees and carefully released the slack in the rope back to the boat. He lifted his hands to his waist and stuck them straight out to show he was skiing with no hands. The girls in the boat squealed and applauded.

Jimmy reached down and retrieved the ski rope handle from behind his knees, pulled it to one side, reached behind his back with his other arm, and performed a spin. The girls squealed and applauded again. Jimmy stepped out of his right ski and used that foot to push down the back of the left ski. As the ski stood up, he started cutting from one side of the wake to the other. He cut out of the wake to the left of the boat, coming almost directly alongside the boat before shifting his weight and cutting across the wake to the right side of the boat. He continued cutting from side to side and jumped the wake of the boat every time he crossed it. After several laps, he made a circling motion in the air with one finger. Ricky recognized the signal and ran him by the peninsula and beached him just as Jimmy had beached him earlier. Ricky circled back to where the ski that Jimmy had dropped was floating. He decelerated and retrieved the ski and pulled in the ski rope. When they circled back toward the boat ramp, they could see Jimmy standing on the dock with a large black inner tube.

"Who wants to ride the tube?" Ricky asked.

Four hands shot in the air. Ricky was not surprised in the slightest. He glided the boat into the dock. Jimmy handed the tube to one of the girls in the front of the boat while steadying the boat, preventing it from hitting the dock. He climbed over the side, and Ricky backed them away from the dock.

Jimmy pulled off his ski vest and held it up. "Who's first?"

Carol, a tanned blonde, took the vest, pulled it on, and fastened the buckles. Ricky stopped in the middle of the lake, where Jimmy tossed the tube over the side and tossed the ski rope handle into the tube. Carol dove out of the boat and swam to the tube. She hoisted herself onto the tube belly down and grabbed the rope. Ricky eased the boat forward and snugged up the slack in the rope.

"Ready?" he hollered. "GO!" she screamed.

Ricky slammed the throttle forward and pulled the tube onto plane before easing back on the throttle. He initiated a zig-zag pattern, slinging the tube across the wake from one side to the other. When the boat reached one end of the lake, he made a sharp turn and laughed as he watched the girl and the tube sliding across the water behind them. A couple laps later, they made another turn, and the girl lost the balance and the tube turned over four or five times, launching her across the lake. Ricky thought she looked like a starfish with her arms and legs spread as she tumbled. He eased the boat over to where she was floating. When pulled alongside her, all they could hear was her laughter. Terri grabbed a ski vest out of the boat, pulled it on, and strapped it. She dove over the side and swam out to the tube. Jimmy pulled in the rope and tossed her the handle. They repeated the process until all the girls had ridden the tube.

Jimmy pulled on a ski vest and dove over the side. He climbed on the tube and grabbed the handle of the ski rope. Ricky laughed.

"Oh, it's on now!" he shouted to the girls in the boat. He slammed the throttle down and jerked Jimmy and the tube out of the water. Once on plane, he did not back off the throttle like he had for the girls. At full throttle, he maneuvered a zig-zag course, making turns much sharper than he had for the girls. Jimmy hung out, dragging one foot then the other to try and control the speeding tube. After a couple laps around the lake, Jimmy was still upright on the tube. Ricky made a cut for the peninsula. He suddenly realized he was closer than he had estimated. When he turned the boat back to the center of the lake, Jimmy and the tube came careening toward the peninsula. The momentum he had built up with the speed of the boat and the angle of the approach sent the tube straight for the side of the peninsula. The tube hit the edge of the shore and flipped sending Jimmy tumbling across the land and into the boat ramp.

"Oh shit!" Ricky hollered, and turned the boat back toward the ramp. He had a sinking feeling in his stomach. Jimmy could have a broken arm or leg or even a serious head wound if he hit the concrete boat ramp.

As they approached, Jimmy crawled onto the dock and shook himself.

"Damn, Hoss!" he said. "I thought you'd killed me there for a second."

"I'm really sorry!" Ricky replied. "Are you alright?" He noticed several scrapes on Jimmy's elbows and knees.

"Yeah," Jimmy replied. "It would take more than that to keep me down."

They tied the boat up to the dock and pulled in the rope. A small crowd was gathered about a hundred yards away at the barbeque grills, and everyone in the boat could smell the aroma of charcoal.

"Let's go eat!" Ricky suggested.

"You don't have to ask me twice!" Jimmy replied as he tossed the ski vest into the boat.

After a dinner of hamburgers and hot dogs, Ricky helped Jimmy load the boat onto the boat trailer and secure the ropes and ski vests.

"Wanna make a lap through Revel and see what's stirring?" Jimmy asked.

"Hell, why not?" Ricky responded.

They both headed into town. When they reached Revel city limits, they headed for the train depot where all the Revel high school kids hung out and rode around. Jimmy and Ricky had ventured down to Revel and rode their circuit a time or two when things were quiet in Haggard. They both knew the traffic pattern and some of the local characters.

They parked in the train depot parking lot, where they spotted Greg, a local boy whose father ran the seafood restaurant just outside of town, at the county line.

"Sup, Greg!" Ricky called out.

"What's happening, Ricky?" Greg replied. "Looks like y'all been doing some waterskiing. That ain't the fishing boat."

Jimmy nodded. "Yeah, one more graduation party."

"Yeah, we had ours down at Pecan Grove Country Club today," Greg continued.

"Nice," Jimmy said. "Did y'all rock the pool off of the high dive?"

Greg laughed. "Of course. Practically drained it we had it rocking so hard. I haven't seen waves that high since the last time I was at the ocean."

"So what's the story with Jenny?" Greg asked, looking at Jimmy.

"Whaddaya mean?" Jimmy replied.

"Well," Greg continued, "I heard tale that you were sweet on her."

"Maybe so," Jimmy answered. "She is pretty cute and has a good sense of humor."

"Then why is she at the Pizza Hut in Haggard with Buck Blue?" Greg asked.

"And how do you know about that?" Jimmy inquired.

"I just happened to be picking up a pizza there earlier and saw them in the corner booth," Greg explained.

"Ain't nobody wearing nobody's ring yet," Jimmy said with a casual shrug that Ricky found less than convincing. "I know I'm not the only one in Whitiker County that's paid her attention."

"You ain't gonna let him slide in there and take her away from you, are ya?" Greg asked.

"Reckon she gets to do the pickin'," Jimmy said. "We ain't going steady. I took her to Dolor last weekend to the movies and to Gargano's for pizza. And I'm pretty sure it was a hell of a lot better pizza than what Pizza Hut turns out. I figure she can go out with Buck if she wants, and she can go out with me. At some point she will make up her mind who she wants to date, and we'll go from there."

"Wow," Greg commented. "You seem pretty at ease with the situation. You ain't jealous she's out with another guy?"

Jimmy laughed. "Let's see. I'm a better shot with a shotgun, rifle, or pistol. I'm a better fisherman. We both ain't much on looks. He don't play guitar and sing. And, I tell better stories. It don't seem like much to worry about, but if it was, there ain't a thing I can do but let her make up her own mind. Now mind you, if she was wearing my class ring and was out with another guy, there'd be a problem. But, it ain't like that-yet."

As Ricky listened to Jimmy talking to Greg, he thought it sounded like Jimmy was trying to talk himself into controlling his jealousy. Ricky was certain that Jimmy was trying to carefully maneuver through maintaining a friendship while yet getting the girl of his dreams. Ricky couldn't help but wonder how this would all play out. He hoped the two wouldn't come to blows over it, and that somehow months from now everyone would still be friends.

Allen Madding

{ 7 }

On Monday morning, Buck Blue was up early, dressed and out the door. He had enjoyed his date with Jenny, and felt like he needed to prove he was steady and reliable. He needed to get a job and start putting some money back so he could move out of his parent's house. He jumped in the Chevelle and headed into town. He drove through downtown and thought how different it all looked on a weekday, when the businesses were open.

He turned onto the highway and continued to the Chevrolet dealership sitting at the edge of town. He parked the Chevelle in a spot outside the service area and walked through the roll-up door. He hung an immediate left and stopped at the door of the service manager.

"Hi, Walt," he said.

Walt looked up from a stack of service tickets and over the top of a pair of reading glasses at Buck.

"Hey, Buck," he replied. "What's going on?"

"I wondered if you had any openings for a mechanic," Buck continued. "Oil change guy, tire man, you name it."

Walt scratched his cheek for a minute while he considered Buck, then responded.

"We could use someone to do oil changes and tire mounting and balancing," he said. "You have some experience working on your own stuff. I can offer you five dollars an hour. Work a while with our certified mechanics, take a few courses, and get your ASE, and we'll get you a raise. How's that sound?"

Buck smiled. "You got yourself a mechanic."

"Ready to start today?" Walt asked.

"Dang skippy!" Buck answered.

"Alright," Walt said, rising from his chair. "Let's walk up front and get Lisa to get your paperwork started."

They walked through the glass door into the showroom and turned in to the offices.

"Hey, Lisa!" Walt called out. "I got a new mechanic that needs to do new-hire paperwork."

"Alright," she said. "Have a seat here, Buck, and we'll get you fixed up."

"When you're done here, come back by my office," Walt said to Buck before walking out of the bookkeeping office.

After Buck completed the stack of forms that Lisa provided him, she got his shirt and pants sizes to order him uniforms.

"OK, Buck," she said. "We're all done here. Your uniforms should be delivered next Friday. Swing by my office every Friday at noon to pick up your paycheck."

"Alrighty!" Buck replied. "Thanks."

Buck stood and walked back to Walt's office. When he reached the doorway, he found Walt wasn't sitting at his desk. He walked to the main shop area and spotted him speaking with a couple mechanics. Walt looked up and saw Buck.

"Hey, Buck!" Walt called. "Come on over."

Buck walked to where the three men stood in front of a new pickup.

"Nice part of a small town is you guys already know each other," Walt noted.

He pointed to the end bay and two-post lift.

"Buck," he continued, "this is your bay for oil changes and tire work."

Buck spent the rest of the day performing oil changes and helping the other mechanics with customer cars.

Just before 5 p.m., Walt stopped by where Buck was cleaning up his area.

"Reckon you'll be back tomorrow?" Walt asked.

Buck laughed. "Yes, sir," he replied. "Ready to rock."

"Are you planning on going to the beach after graduation?" Walt asked.

"Well," Buck answered, "didn't think I should ask for time off just starting a job."

Walt smiled. "It'll be alright. You only graduate from high school once. You can have next week off. We work till noon on Saturdays. Work this week and take next week to go to the beach with your friends. We'll have plenty for you to do when you return," he said.

"Thanks!" Buck replied.

Buck finished cleaning up his area and putting away tools. He washed up, then helped close the garage roll-up doors.

"See you in the morning, Buck," Walt said.

{ 8 }

Ricky Mann was sitting at the edge of field, servicing the generator and pump, when he saw a white pickup approaching. He finished checking the oil on both engines, and filled the fuel tanks from the auxiliary tank mounted in the bed of his pickup. Once both tanks were filled, he shut off the pump on the tank on his truck and hung up the nozzle. He pulled a red shop rag from the hip pocket of his jeans and wiped his hands as his father pulled up.

"Hey Ricky," his father called out.

"What's up, Pop?" Ricky replied.

"Your mom and I have been talking and wanted you to consider something," his father continued.

"OK," Ricky said.

"Since you intend to work on the farm now that you're graduating high school, how 'bout considering going over to ABAC and workin' on an associate's degree in agriculture? I've taught you about as much as I know, but we've been thinking you could bring a lot to the business side of the operation by taking some of the courses they teach," his father explained.

"OK," Ricky said slowly, raising an eyebrow. "But how would I pay for that? College classes ain't cheap."

His father nodded in agreement. "Your mom has researched the cost, and here's what we came up with You pass your classes and complete your degree in two years, and the farm will pay for your schooling."

Ricky stared down at the Georgia clay ground and silently considered the offer. Did he want to spend the rest of his life here on the farm? If not, what else was he going to do? He didn't have money for college to pursue some other career, and there wasn't a load of career opportunities here. He wiped his hands on the shop rag again and looked up at his father.

"I'd say we got a deal," Ricky said. "I'll ride over to Tifton and see what it takes to get registered."

"Alright," his father replied. "Talk to your mom, and she'll give you a check."

Rick's father started his pickup and left in a cloud of dust. Ricky returned his attention to the irrigation system. He started the generator and the pump. Water squirted from all of the spray nozzles as the water pressure built, and finally the end gun was pulsating water. He walked over to the center tower on the irrigation system and threw the switch to start the motors that made the system gradually rotate, or "walk." He paused for a few minutes, watching the system operate and reviewing the gauges on the generator and pump engines, before easing into his pickup to head to the next irrigation system one field over.

Allen Madding

{9}

On Saturday morning, Buck was finishing a customer's oil change when, out of the corner of his eye, he noticed Walt walking his direction.

"Hey Buck!" he called as he approached. "Mrs. Hamilton has brought her car in with two complaints. Wanna give it an inspection when you're done with this oil change?"

"Sure," Buck answered as he lowered the lift.

Buck checked the oil level in the customer's car, made a few notes on the work order, wiped his hands on an orange shop rag from his back pocket, and walked the service order to the bins hanging outside the door of Walt's office. He walked back to his service bay and sat down in the driver's seat of the customer's car. He started the engine and glanced down at the dash. When all of the warning lights went off, he dropped the shifter into reverse and carefully backed the car out of the bay and drove it out of the garage to the parking lot. He parked the car and stopped at Walt's office and hung the keys on the key rack next to the work order bins.

Buck looked at the waiting work order in the bin with Mrs. Hamilton's name at the top. In the box labeled "Customer Complaint," he read a handwritten summary: "soft brakes and water light remains on even after filling."

Buck took the service order and the attached key ring and walked out to the parking lot. He found Mrs. Hamilton's burgundy 1976 Buick Electra 225, a car with a back seat as big as the sofa in his parent's living room and a trunk Buck was convinced could hold eight dead bodies. He sat down under the steering wheel of the mammoth sedan and cranked the engine. The big 455-cubic-inch V-8 roared to life, and Buck noted the water warning light was illuminated. He pressed the brake pedal with his foot to pull the shifter into reverse and noted the brake pedal almost went to the floor and did not feel firm like it should.

He pulled the land yacht of a car into his stall and across the lift. He shut the car off and raised the hood. He inspected the heater hoses and radiator hoses. He tilted his head a bit and inspected the water pump gasket where it was bolted to the front of the engine block. He recognized that the engine was too hot to open the radiator cap.

While he waited for the engine to cool, he moved on to the brake issues. He popped the retaining spring latch on the brake master cylinder reservoir to check the brake fluid level. He pulled the lid off the reservoir, and it appeared full. But as he was about to put the lid back, he stopped, furrowing his brow. He glanced back at the brake fluid. It seemed clearer than normal. An idea started to form, and he stuck a finger in the fluid and held his finger to his nose. Sure enough, no brake-fluid scent. And it didn't feel greasy. He pushed down the sense of satisfaction in realizing the problem. Better not tell Walt until he completed a more thorough check.

Buck stepped back and knelt down and positioned the lift arms under the car. Once he had the lift arms positioned underneath the car's frame, he walked over to the air-control lever. With a tug of the lever, the lift gently raised the behemoth car. One the car was high enough to walk under, Buck heard the clinking sound of the safety locks falling into place. He released his grip on the valve and walked under the car to inspect the brake lines and hoses. As he looked up, a drop of rusty water fell from the brake lines to his nose.

In southwest Georgia, it rarely ever snowed. The roads were never salted; thus the sight of rusted metal brake lines was a bit odd—even on a six-year-old car that had twelve thousand miles on it. Buck walked out from under the car and lowered it back to the floor. He patted the radiator cap and determined it was cool enough to remove so he could peer into the radiator: it had no water that he could see, but it was dark. He walked over to his toolbox and retrieved a flashlight. He stepped back to the car and shined the flashlight into the radiator. It was about half full.

Buck turned off the flashlight, placed it back in his toolbox, and headed to Walt's office. When he reached the doorway, he spotted Walt at the parts counter, chatting with the parts manager.

"Walt. Do you have a second?" Buck asked.

"Sure, Buck," Walt responded. "Whatcha got?"

Buck explained what he found. "And it seems to me that the master cylinder is full of water," he finished.

Walt wrinkled his forehead. "Water in the brakes?" he asked.

"Yeah," Buck said. "Come take a look."

At Buck's service bay, he walked Walt through the steps he'd taken.

"I'll be damned," Walt said. "I don't think I've ever seen brake lines rusted like this on a car that has been actively driven."

Buck nodded.

"Let's see how extensive the damage is. Pull a rear wheel and drum, and let's take a look at the wheel cylinder," Walt recommended.

Buck grabbed a screwdriver and pulled the hubcap off one rear wheel. He pulled an air impact wrench and a socket from his toolbox and connected it to an air hose. He removed five lug nuts and bounced the wheel and tire to the shop floor He clicked an adjuster on the brake backing plate until he could pull the brake drum off. He laid the brake drum down on the shop floor, and they both peered up to the wheel cylinder. The wheel cylinder was a big, leaking ball of rust.

"Water in the brakes," Buck reported.

Walt shook his head. "Let me talk with her," he said. He turned and ambled toward the showroom.

After a few minutes, Walt came walking across the shop with Mrs. Hamilton in tow. He led her to the car and stopped at the front fender on the driver's side.

"Mrs. Hamilton, would you show me where you have been adding water?" Walt asked.

"Sure," the old woman answered.

She walked over to where Walt was standing, stretched out a crooked finger, and pointed to the brake master cylinder.

"Right there," she said. "I flip that bailing wire over, pull that lid off, and fill it. It usually ain't very low, and the darn water light won't go out."

"Yes, ma'am," Walt replied. "That's because that's where the brake fluid goes."

He pointed over at the radiator cap and the surge tank on the fender.

"That is where the water goes," he continued. "The radiator is low on water and the brake lines are all rusted from the water. So we need to replace the lower radiator hose and refill the radiator. Then we need to drain the brake system, replace all of the brake lines and the wheel cylinders and calipers so the brakes work properly again."

"Oh!" the old woman sheepishly replied. "How long is that gonna take?"

"Well, we close at noon because it's Saturday," Walt stated. "We can get started on all this Monday. I'd say we should have it back to you at the end of the day Tuesday, noon Wednesday at the latest."

"Alright," she said. "Let me call my daughter to come pick me up."

"Yes, ma'am," Walt answered, and led her back to the showroom to use the phone.

Buck looked up at the clock on the wall over the walk-in door to the parking lot and saw it was approaching noon. He cleaned up his tools, put them in the toolbox, and locked it. He grabbed a broom and swept his stall.

Shortly, Walt walked back into the garage and rolled down the garage doors. He walked over and met Buck near his stall.

"Well, Buck," he said, "enjoy your weekend, graduation, and the beach. We'll see you a week from Monday."

"Thanks, Walt," Buck replied. "Have a good weekend."

Buck washed his hands in the mop sink at one end of the garage before walking out to the Chevelle. He drove south to the Dairy Queen and pulled into one of the remaining parking spots. The parking lot was almost at capacity, and the drive-through line surrounded the red brick building. He walked into the building and got in line for the register. There were about ten people in front of him. Haggard's restaurant options were somewhat limited, and the Dairy Queen seemed popular on Saturdays. Emmy Lou, a tired gray-haired woman, stood at the register, writing orders on a paper tablet and ringing them up on the register. There was no hurry in her process. She tore a small strip with the order number and total off the bottom of the tablet and handed it to the customer before hanging the order on a metal strip in the divider between her and the kitchen. She turned and filled a wax cup with Dairy Queen's mascot, Dennis the Menace, on the side with crushed ice, and poured a Coke, deliberately put a lid on it, and handed it to the customer.

Buck stood and watched the sluggish process repeat itself ten times. As he stood and watched, he wondered how many orders

Emmy Lou had recorded over the years. As long as he could re-member, she'd been at the register taking orders. Finally, the last person in line in front of him got their order number slip and Coke and stepped to the left to wait for their meal.

"Hi, Miss Emmy Lou," Buck greeted her.

"Hello, Buck," she said without any noticeable enthusiasm. "What ya having?"

"Give me a chicken tender basket with white gravy and a cherry vanilla Coke," Buck said.

Emmy Lou scribbled the order on the tablet and rang it up on the register. "That'll be $3.76."

Buck handed her a five-dollar bill. She punched it into the reg-ister and the cash drawer popped open. She counted out his change to him, ripped the strip off the bottom of the order tab-let, handed it to him, and hung the order on the metal divider behind her. She grabbed another wax cup, filled it with crushed ice, reached above the Coke dispenser, and added two pumps of cherry flavoring and two pumps of vanilla flavoring into the cup before filling it with Coke. She put a lid on it and set it on the counter in front of him. He picked up the Coke and grabbed a straw and stuck it through the lid.

There was no one else in line behind Buck. Emmy Lou drew a breath and relaxed while the back line prepared the orders.

"How ya been, Miss Emmy Lou?" Buck asked.

"I been better," she reported. "I gots these bunions on my foots. So I has to wear my fluffy house shoes to work. I can't barely walk. And these folks all wanting their food like we have some fast turnaround about to make me lose my mind. I'm working for two dolla' and fifty cent an hour while they're complaining about how fast a cheeseburger gets cooked."

Buck nodded, regretting he had asked.

The cook behind the divider rang a bell. Emmy Lou turned to retrieve an order.

"One-three-six!" she called out.

A customer raised his hand and took the tray of food from her. She continued to retrieve orders and call numbers. Buck watched, thinking that it had to be mind-numbing work. Shortly she called One-forty-five, and Buck took his order to a red wooden booth to sit.

Buck finished his lunch and dumped his tray in the red trash can by the door to the parking lot and dropped the empty tray on top of the trash can's lid.

"Y'all be good!" Emmy Lou called out to him as he headed out the door, still sipping on his vanilla cherry Coke.

Buck slid in behind the wheel of the Chevelle and fired up the
V-8. He sat the Coke between his legs and pulled the car into
gear. He drove to his family's modest white clapboard-sided
one-story house with a large front porch nestled beneath large
oak and magnolia trees just south of town and parked under a
sprawling oak tree in the backyard. He ambled across the yard
and into the house, letting the screen door bang shut from the
tension of the long spring that ran diagonally across it. The
house was quiet as his father worked six days a week driving a
truck, his mother was gone cleaning a couple houses, and his
brother was off somewhere on his bicycle. He stepped into the
living room and turned on the television. He turned the dial and
found Georgia Championship Wrestling. He plopped down in a
rocking chair to watch the weekly antics of "The American
Dream" Dusty Rhodes, Ole Anderson, Tommy "Wildfire" Rich,
Abdullah the Butcher, the Great Kabuki, "The Nature Boy" Ric
Flair, and Roddy Piper.

After getting his weekly fix of wrestling, Buck went out to the
backyard. He began washing the Chevelle methodically, working from the roof down to the windows while thinking about
Jenny and how he could win her affections once and for all.
Once the roof and windows had been washed, he rinsed them.
He moved on to washing the hood and trunk and again rinsed
the car. Meticulously, he moved his attention to the front grill
and front bumper; then he moved down the driver side of the

car, washing from the top to the bottom and again rinsing. He moved to the rear taillights and bumper before moving onto the passenger side of the car. Once it was rinsed, he washed the wheels and the sidewalls of the tires. Once completed, he dumped the bucket and rinsed it out, setting it upside down by the back steps of the house. He rinsed out the sponge and set it on top of the bucket to dry in the sun. He walked to the clothes-line beside the house and grabbed a chamois cloth. He sprayed it with water until it became soft and rang it out with his hands. He walked to the Chevelle and dried the roof, ringing out the excess water from the chamois and drying the windows. He con-tinued the process until the car was completely dry and spotless. He rinsed the chamois cloth, rung it out, and hung it back on the clothesline. He shut off the water faucet and dropped the garden hose nozzle next to the faucet.

Buck checked his watch. Several families had gone together to rent out the American Legion swimming pool for a senior party, and he had been invited. He headed in the house, took a quick shower, and changed into swimming shorts, T-shirt, and a pair of tennis shoes. He walked back out to the waiting Chevelle and drove into town. Once on Broad Street, he turned onto the road leading to the city water tower on one side and the American Legion on the other. He turned and parked, recognizing Ricky and Jimmy's trucks parked nearby.

He walked up to the chain-link gate and stepped into the pool area. The jukebox that normally set just inside the snack bar was sitting on the porch facing the pool area. He saw Ricky, Jimmy, and a handful of other kids from school playing volleyball to his right. A large barbeque grill was set up to his left with smoke rolling out of it. Buck guessed from the smell that it was hot dogs and hamburgers. He looked across the Olympic-sized pool toward the high dive and the huge slide. As Mary, a gorgeous blonde-headed girl from the gymnastics team in a bikini, slid down the slide and launched into the pool, one of his classmates' mothers called his name.

"Hey Buck," she called. "There's a big cooler near the grill full of drinks. Help yourself. Dinner will be ready shortly."

He silently nodded in acknowledgment and continued to casually look around the pool, noting who was there and who wasn't. He noted Jenny wasn't present and hoped she would be coming. He walked to the cooler, flipped the top open, and retrieved an ice-cold RC Cola and pulled the pop top on it.

He walked over to the jukebox and made a selection. After a series of noises, Waylon Jennings was singing "Mamas Don't Let Your Babies Grow Up to Be Cowboys." Immediately, all the guys playing volleyball were singing along. Buck grinned and walked back to the baby pool area, which was divided from the rest of the massive pool by a short concrete wall topped with chain-link fence. He stepped into the shallow water and sat down on the bottom of the pool and leaned back against the side of the pool and relaxed, drinking his RC and listening to the music.

Shortly, Ricky and Jimmy joined him. Buck noted Jimmy's drink was in a Styrofoam surround. He chuckled.

"What ya enjoying there, Jimmy?" he asked knowingly. "Bet it ain't an RC."

Jimmy held the concealed can in the air and grinned a devious grin.

"Busch!" he said holding the "sh" sound out so long it sounded like a balloon deflating.

"I didn't see those in the cooler!" Buck protested.

"You didn't look in the right cooler," Jimmy pointed out. He nodded toward the side of the porch. On the ground just below where the jukebox sat and out of direct line of sight set a cooler that Buck recognized as belonging to Jimmy from the distinctive Waylon Jennings Flying W decal on the side.

Buck laughed. "I shoulda known."

Jimmy grinned. "There's a couple more of these Styrofoam insulators in the cooler to keep 'em cold."

Buck laughed again. "Yeah. Cold and incognito."

Jimmy laughed. "Precisely."

The conversation immediately stopped as all three guys saw Jenny walking through the gate wearing a T-shirt and white shorts. Jimmy noted a smile break out on Buck's face. She looked around the area until her gaze fell on the three guys sitting in the baby pool. She shook her head and walked to the edge.

"Y'all mean to tell me the three of you graduated high school and are still required to stay in the baby pool?" she asked with a smirk.

Jimmy laughed. "We're keeping Buck company. He looked scared and alone over here."

"Buck, do you want me to get you a life jacket?" she asked.

"No," he replied. "But if you wanna grab me a cold..."

Jimmy cut him off midsentence. "Spinach!" he interjected. "A cold spinach."

Jenny shook her head. "You heathens brought a cooler, didn't you?"

Jimmy smiled. "You bet that anywhere I am there's a cooler with cold spinach close by."

Jenny laughed. "Cold spinach."

She spotted Jimmy's cooler nestled below the jukebox and made her way to it, flipped it open, slid a beer in a Styrofoam insulator, closed the lid, and walked back to where the guys sat. She pulled the pop top on the beer and took a long sip.

"That was mine!" Buck protested.

"Says who?" Jenny asked, taking another sip.

"I asked you to get me one," he explained.

"Oh that," she said. "Yours is still in the cooler, sport. Get your own."

"OOOOOH!" Jimmy and Ricky yelled simultaneously.

"Food's ready!" one of the parents called from the grill.

Everyone descended on the grill area and started piling food on plates. Some sat at the picnic tables, while others sat on the grass and on the porch steps. Ricky quietly observed the crowd, noting who was here, who was noticeably absent, and who brought guests. He noticed Matt Decker had brought Terri Young, a gorgeous brunette with olive skin wearing a string bikini.

Matt and Terri sat at the next picnic table over, so Terri caught Ricky's eye when she got up—alone—to toss her paper plate and go to the pool. Matt went back to the court. Ricky found it odd—if he were there with a girl like Terri, he'd never leave her side—but whatever, not his business.

When Ricky finished eating, he tossed his trash into a nearby trash can. He walked over to Jimmy's cooler, grabbed a beer, and slid it into a foam insulator. He strolled back to the pool and sat down on the side with his feet in the water. He thought back to when he was five years old taking swimming lessons in this very area of the huge pool.

Suddenly, Terri emerged from the water about 6 feet in front of him. As she flung her hair out of her face, he noticed her bikini top had slipped down on one side, revealing one of her breasts.

"Hey, Ricky!" she said, oblivious to her exposure.

Ricky tried to remain cool and keep his eyes on her beautiful face, not her beautiful, well— Should he tell her?

"Hi, Terri," he replied nonchalantly.

"Figured out what you're doing this fall?" she asked.

"Yeah. I'm gonna go to ABAC and work on the farm," he answered.

When it became apparent she wasn't going to notice, he decided to tell her.

"Terri, pull your top up," he advised.

She looked down at her exposed breast and squealed. "Ricky!"

She pulled her top up and swiftly swam away.

"And the end of another pleasant conversation," he said to himself, regretting that he hadn't phrased things more delicately to hopefully save Terri a tiny bit of embarrassment, while still holding onto the image.

As the sun set, one of the parents called everyone to the picnic tables where they were greeted with a large ice cream cake from the Dairy Queen that had "Congratulations Class of '82" written on it in icing.

After everyone polished off the ice cream cake, they initiated their departures. Ricky noticed in the distance the figures of Matt and Terri quietly headed to his Mustang.

Jimmy, Buck, and Jenny came walking up behind him. Everyone had changed from swimsuits into street clothes.

"We're headed to the OK Corral," Jimmy announced as he tossed his cooler in the back of his pickup.

"Yeah. Sounds like a plan," Ricky responded.

Buck, Jimmy, Ricky, and Jenny reconvened at the city parking lot like they did many weekend nights. But this night had a different air about it. Tomorrow they would graduate from high school and start a new chapter in their lives.

Around midnight, Jimmy interrupted the flow of conversation with a proposal.

"It's our last night as high school seniors," he noted.

"No shit, Sherlock," Buck replied dryly.

Jimmy paid no attention to his response. "We need to celebrate this occasion in grand style," he continued.

"What exactly do you have in mind, cowboy?" asked Jenny.

"Let's climb the water tower!" Jimmy suggested. "We can park with the American Legion crowd.If the cops ride through they won't suspect anything."

"I'm in," Ricky responded.

Buck nodded. "Hell yeah!"

Jenny shook her head. "I'll keep my feet on the ground. You boys go have your fun."

"You sure?" Jimmy needled her.

"Yeah. Y'all have fun. I'm going home and going to bed," she answered.

Ricky noticed the slight disappointment in the faces of both Buck and Jimmy at her response. But as expected, Jimmy tried to play it off.

"Suit yourself," Jimmy replied. "Let's roll, boys!"

The three guys piled in Jimmy's truck. He cranked the engine
and they headed out South Broad street to the American Legion. When they arrived, they could hear the band playing
Lynyrd Skynyrd's "Sweet Home Alabama." The parking lot held
a couple rows of cars. Jimmy pulled in alongside a car in the second row. They set silently looking around. They saw no moving
cars and no one moving outside. With the coast clear, they exited the truck and made their way to the chain-link fence surrounding the water tower.

Jimmy went first. He went to one of the corner of the fenced en-
closure and scaled the fence with ease. When he reached the top,
he grabbed the top of the corner post and hurled himself over
the barbed wire lining the top with the level of skill and dexterity of someone who had performed this technique numerous
times in the past. Buck rapidly followed, taking a bit more time
to successfully cross the barbed wire. Then Ricky. With all
three guys inside the fence, Jimmy grabbed the bottom rung of
the ladder on the side of the water tower, pulled himself up, and
ascended the 130 feet to the top. Buck followed a few rungs behind, and Ricky bought up the rear. After several minutes of
quiet climbing, they each reached the top—somewhat winded
but in good shape.

Jimmy walked down the deck a few feet and stopped, facing the handrail and looking out across the horizon.

"Boys, I need to get rid of a few beers," he announced.

He unzipped his jeans and urinated off the side of the water tower. After a few minutes, he shook his hand a few times and zipped his pants up. After what seemed like a minute later, Ricky heard the stream hit the ground below.

"Damn!" Jimmy exclaimed. "You know you're high up when you can pee and zip up before it hits the ground."

Buck shook his head. "It's a regular science experiment over here," he noted as he spit tobacco juice over the rail.

The guys stood silent for a few minutes, taking in the scenery surrounding them. Buck reached into one of the many pockets on his camouflage pants.

"Who's up for a beer?"

Jimmy's head snapped toward Buck. "Where'd you get that?"

Buck chuckled. "These camo pants have a bunch of cargo pockets that are just the right size."

He tossed a beer to Jimmy. Jimmy popped the top and shook his head. "I hereby dub thee Cap'n Beerpants."

Ricky laughed. "Hey, Cap'n Beerpants, toss one my way."

Buck dug a beer out of another pocket and tossed it to him. Ricky popped the top.

As he drew a sip, he saw movement in the long driveway leading from Broad Street below. "Everybody quiet and stand still!" Ricky hissed.

All three stared down at a black-and-white Ford Fairmont easing its way up the long driveway. Haggard Police was a pretty small department. The guys knew there were only two cars patrolling, and they knew each of the officers by name. If they were caught, they could be charged with trespassing, public intoxication, and—in Ricky's case—underage drinking. The patrol car gradually rode between the rows of parked cars, shining its spotlight across the parking light. The spotlight went out as the patrol car made a circle around the legs of the water tower and headed back down the driveway toward Broad Street.

Buck let out a long sigh. "Close call."

The guys finished their beers, crushed the cans, and slid them in their pockets so they'd leave no evidence behind. Jimmy was the first one to the ladder. "Alright. Let's get going."

Ricky started down the long ladder. When he was halfway down, Jimmy started to follow. When Ricky reached the last rung of the ladder, he hopped down to the ground. He looked up to see Jimmy halfway down and Buck at the top of the ladder.

Ricky ambled to the corner of the chain-link fence and surveyed the surroundings. No cops in sight. He climbed up the fence, over the barbed wire, and down the other side. After a few minutes, Jimmy made his way over the fence with Buck close behind.

The guys climbed back into the pickup and headed back to the city parking lot. On the way, Jimmy looked over at Ricky and Buck. "You know, guys, we need to pick up a couple special guests for tomorrow's graduation ceremony. I know they'd hate to miss it."

Buck glanced at Jimmy and raised an eyebrow. "What do you have in mind?"

Jimmy flashed a devious grin. "You'll understand soon enough." He looked at Ricky. "Grab your truck. We'll need two. Let's go to Dolor."

{ 10 }

A s Ricky approached Whitiker County High School, he glanced up at the front of the entrance to the cafeteria and gymnasium and grinned. Standing atop the roof were Ronald McDonald and the Shoney's Big Boy. He pulled his pickup into the student parking. He scanned the lot and noted that Jimmy's truck and Buck's Chevelle were already parked. Ricky was surprised to see the Butts boys' truck sitting in the parking lot. "Wow, are those two actually graduating?" he thought. He grabbed his cap and gown off the truck's bench seat and strolled to the main lobby entrance. He smiled as he recognized this would be his last trip into the school as a high school student. When he reached the cafeteria, all of the seniors were sitting at tables conversing. He plopped down in a chair at the table where Jimmy, Buck, and Jenny were seated. Before he had a chance to speak to them, the school's principal banged on a table with his palm.

"Alright. Y'all give me your attention for a minute. We were surprised to see two guests greeting us from the roof when we arrived at the school this morning. If anyone has any information on how they got there or where they came from, the Haggard Police would like to hear from you."

He looked around the room but could not make eye contact with any of the seniors, so he continued. "Y'all have practiced marching in, so try to remember what the teachers told you. When you march in, keep about two to three feet between you and the person in front of you. You'll be lined up by the rows where you are going to be seated.

"Pay attention when we call the scholarships. Nothing looks worse than me having to call your name four or five times, and your neighbor having to elbow you to get your attention to come get your scholarship. When we get to the time to award diplomas, each row will rise and walk forward. You'll take your diploma in your left hand and shake my hand with your right hand. You'll walk across the platform, stop in front of the photographer, have your picture taken, and then return to your seat trying to carefully pay attention and not fall off the stage. Try to act like you have some sense about you and don't embarrass your parents any more than you already have over the last twelve years." He directed a pointed look toward Ricky and crew and then to the Butts boys.

"After the ceremonies have concluded, you're invited to the parking lot to toss your caps in the air. Don't toss your caps in the gymnasium. In a couple minutes, your homeroom teachers will escort you to their rooms to put on your caps and gowns. You'll stay there until they escort you back here to line up to march into the gymnasium."

Ricky looked across the table to see Jimmy cleaning his finger-
nails with his pocket knife. He was pretty sure Jimmy hadn't
paid any attention to the principal's long speech. The senior
class resumed their conversations as soon as the principal ended
his speech. Jimmy closed his pocket knife, slid it back into his
pants pocket, and looked up at Ricky.

"Did you hear what happened with Carol Wilson last night?"

Ricky shook his head. "No. What?"

Jimmy nodded. "You know her boyfriend has that Trans Am he
waxed Buck with a month or so ago. Well, he was carrying her
home last night, and the Haggard Police tried to pull him over
for speeding as he was headed out. He decided he wasn't gonna
stop for them, so he ran for the city limits. Their little Ford
Fairmont couldn't keep up. So, he thought he was in the clear,
ran down past the school here and took a turn at the county line
to take her home a little too hot. He blew the right front tire in
the middle of the turn and slid off in the ditch. Super Trooper
Officer Swisher came rolling up a few minutes later, blue lights
and siren on, in a so-called high-speed pursuit—considering a
Fairmont probably tops out around seventy."

Ricky's eyes widened. "Anyone hurt?"

"Oh my God!" Jenny exclaimed at the same time. "Is Carol alright?"

Jimmy shook his head. "Everyone's fine. But Officer Swisher handcuffed him and Carol went off on Swisher for handcuffing a guy after having an accident. Swisher started in about outrunning them, high-speed pursuit, yada yada. She told him that she hadn't seen any blue lights or heard any sirens. Her boyfriend was just in a hurry to get her home before curfew. Super cop was thinking he was going to get a gold star or something. His sergeant came out, listened to Swisher's story and Carol's story, and asked Swisher if he realized he was five miles out of his jurisdiction. So Swisher starts in again about high-speed pursuit. His sergeant tells him that he hadn't received authorization for any high-speed pursuit, he wasn't Buford T. Justice, and he wasn't living out a scene from Smokey and the Bandit."

Jenny, Ricky, and Buck broke out laughing.

Ricky smirked and shook his head. "Poor old Officer Swisher. Reckon they'll have him on foot rattling doors again?"

Jimmy grinned. "More than likely!"

Ray Smith walked up to the table where they were seated. Ricky recognized him as one of the kids from the neighboring Butcher County. This was the first year Whitiker and Butcher Counties had joined together and opened this new high school building. While Whitiker County was a dry county that only sold beer and wine, Butcher County set just the other side of the river a few miles away and sold all forms of liquor. Ray's father owned one of the two liquor stores just on the other side of the bridge. Despite the two counties' differences on alcohol sales, neither sold alcohol on Sunday, and the school system had seen fit to schedule graduation on a Sunday afternoon.

"Hey y'all. My dad sent us all a graduation present. The trunk of my Thunderbird is filled with champagne, tequila, whiskey, and vodka. He even sent toasting glasses for the champagne. Stop by as you leave and pick out a bottle as your gift. I'll open the champagne so everyone can have a glass."

Jimmy smiled. "Thanks, Ray. Tell your dad we appreciate it and will return the favor with our business."

Ray nodded and walked to the next table.

Shortly, the homeroom teachers appeared and called them to their rooms. Everyone pulled on the caps and gowns. The senior boys had been instructed to wear a white shirt, black pants, and black dress shoes. Jimmy, Ricky, and Buck had complied to the greatest extent of their abilities. Each one was wearing a white dress shirt, black pants, and black cowboy boots.

Shortly, the teachers led them to the cafeteria and lined them up by classroom to prepare to march into the gym. Ricky took a peek and was amazed to see the stands were packed. He spotted his parents seated by the door. His mom was holding his Resistol straw cowboy hat in her lap. As "Pomp and Circumstance" played, the seniors marched into the gym; each class turned down their respective aisle and stood in front of their metal folding chairs. After the principal said his piece and a local pastor said a prayer, they were seated and prepared to listen to the monotony of speeches by the valedictorian, salutatorian, and guest speaker. Jimmy was seated three seats down from Ricky. Jimmy pulled out a deck of playing cards and dealt poker to the four in the row. Quietly, they began to play their hands while ignoring the speakers on the platform.

After two hands of poker, the speeches concluded and the principal awarded scholarships. Jimmy dealt a third hand of poker. Ricky was studying his hand of cards when the girl to his right nudged him and told him to go get his award.

Ricky chuckled. "Yeah, right. Like I am gonna fall for that gag."

The principal looked out at the seniors. "Ricky Mann, please come forward to accept the PTA scholarship."

Shocked that he'd received a scholarship, Ricky jumped up, tossed his cards in his seat, and bolted for the aisle. He regained his composure on his way to the platform. He walked up the steps, crossed the platform to where the principal was standing at the podium waiting for him. He accepted the envelope with his left hand and shook the principal's hand with his right.

The principal leaned over his shoulder and whispered in his ear. "Nice going, Jackass. Put the cards up and pay attention," he said with a slight chuckle.

Ricky smiled and nodded as he dropped his hand and walked across the platform to the exit stairs. He returned to his seat while trying to suppress laughter. The seniors on his row slapped his back and congratulated him on his way through.

"Just like Jimmy to get me in trouble on the final day in this place," Ricky thought to himself with a chuckle.

When they concluded with the awards, the principal asked the first row of seniors to stand and approach the platform. As he called their names one by one, they crossed the platform, shook his hand, accepted their diploma, and returned to their row. When Buck's name was called, Jimmy stuck two fingers in his teeth and whistled, while Ricky hooped and hollered. Once every senior had returned to their row, they sat back down together. The pattern continued until Jimmy and Ricky found themselves in line at the edge of the platform.

Jimmy looked over his shoulder at Ricky. "Reckon there is really a diploma in ours, or just an empty folder?"

Ricky chuckled. "Well, since they gave me the PTA scholarship, I guess at least I am getting a diploma. You, on the other hand— all bets are off."

Jimmy chuckled.

All joking aside, Jimmy was a pretty intelligent guy who enjoyed reading as much as he did the great outdoors. High school had come pretty easy to him, and he had rocked along with a 3.0 grade point average without a lot of work. Ricky on the other hand had struggled with math and applying himself to history classes.

Shortly, their names were called. They processed through the drill like everyone else and returned to their seats. Discreetly, Jimmy and Ricky cracked open the leather folders, confirmed they had diplomas in them, and each gave a thumbs-up.

After working through the class of two hundred students, the principal asked the seniors to stand. Music played, and they marched out to the cafeteria. As Ricky passed his parents, he took his cowboy hat from his mother. He took his mortarboard cap off and put on his cowboy hat as they proceeded to the parking lot. The class gathered and tossed their caps in the air. The seniors milled around while family sought them out to give hugs and congratulations.

Ricky's mom appeared from the crowd. "OK, hot shot. Why didn't you go up to get your scholarship the first time they called you?"

Ricky grinned. "I was a little distracted and wasn't listening."

His dad chuckled. "That sounds like a recap of your entire high school experience."

Ricky laughed. "It's all Jimmy's fault. He had me engaged in a game of poker."

Jimmy threw his hands in the air. "Whoa, whoa, whoa! I didn't hold a gun to your head and force you to play poker. And besides, it's not my fault you can't play poker and listen at the same time!"

Ricky's father laughed. "I don't suppose you guys know anything about the Shoney's Big Boy and the Ronald McDonald on top of the school."

Ricky raised his eyebrows. "I plead the fifth."

Ricky's mother smiled. "Well, he did learn something in the American Government class, I guess!"

"Yup," Ricky answered automatically.

His mom must have sensed he was antsy to get going. "You boys don't stay out too late. You have a senior breakfast at eight in the morning and a long drive to the beach tomorrow."

Ricky smiled. "Yes, ma'am."

Ricky and Jimmy made their way out to the student parking lot and located Ray Smith's Thunderbird. Ray was just a few steps behind them. Ray opened the trunk and filled plastic glasses with champagne and handed them out. A small crowd of about a dozen seniors, several of whom were still seventeen, raised their glasses and sipped champagne on a Sunday in a dry county in the Bible Belt, saluting an end to a chapter in their lives and their first step into adulthood.

{ 11 }

After nearly four hours of driving the next day, Ricky arrived at Panama City Beach. He had not made any reservations as his plans and budget didn't include accommodations like the Holiday Inn overlooking the Gulf of Mexico. Instead he opted for a budget twenty-room one-story motor lodge that did not have a swimming pool sitting on the other side of Front Beach Road. Ricky figured what he saved on the room he could use for food and drinks. Once he checked in and tossed a duffle bag of clothes on the bed, he pulled on a bathing suit and slipped his bare feet into a pair of Converse tennis shoes. He climbed into his pickup and headed down Front Beach Road.

The smell of salt water filled the cab of the truck, and Ricky basked in the smell, the glimpses of the beach, the girls in bikinis walking along on the sidewalk, and the warmth of the sun. He hadn't been riding very long when he spotted a familiar sky-blue Chevy pickup with a Waylon Jennings Flying W flag waving from a pole mounted in the pickup bed turning in to the parking lot of the Bikini Beach Resort.

He turned in behind the truck and parked beside it, then shouted, "What's up, Jimmy! Like the new flag!"

Jimmy's head spun toward the sound.

"How the hell did you find me so fast?" Jimmy exclaimed.

"Pure luck I guess," Ricky responded.

Ricky noticed the bed of Jimmy's truck contained a tarp covering a large rectangular shape—much larger than a cooler or anything else he'd expect in his friend's truck. "What the hell is under the tarp?" he asked, brows furrowed in consideration.

Jimmy's eyes darted around the parking lot. No one was in earshot.

"Well," he began, "I was driving along this morning and wanted a Coke or something, and I hadn't packed any. I stopped at a gas station just at the Georgia-Florida border that hadn't opened yet, but that had vending machines outside. The dang Coke machine took my money, but no Coke. I pushed every button on the darn thing—nothing. I tried the coin return—still nothing. So I did what any red-blooded south Georgia boy would do. I backed up to the Coke machine and loaded it on the truck. I drove a couple miles, opened it with my crowbar, and got me a Coke. Wanna Coke?"

Ricky shook his head and laughed. "I would have opened it with a crowbar and got my Coke. I don't think I'da taken the whole damned machine!"

Jimmy shrugged his shoulders. "Seemed like the right thing at the time. I was pissed!"

Ricky continued to laugh. "OK. So now what are you gonna do with it?"

Jimmy grinned. "Pass out drinks and quarters? Let me get checked in and toss my bag in the room. We need to go get some beer."

Ricky nodded. "I'd recommend being discreet on the dispersion of drinks and quarters. You don't want to have to try to explain this to the local law."

Jimmy nodded. "Good point."

Jimmy headed into the lobby while Ricky sat in his truck listening to the new .38 Special cassette. While he was waiting, he heard a car come into the driveway and turned to see Buck's Chevelle pulling in a couple spots over.

Ricky stepped out of the truck and over to greet him. "What's up, Buck?" he said as he approached the car.

"Hey Ricky! Where's Jimmy?"

"He's inside checking in," Ricky responded.

"Cool. I saw the truck and the Waylon flag, I figured it couldn't be anyone else. Me and my little brother are staying down at the Trade Winds."

"Alright," Ricky replied. "Soon as Jimmy's settled here, we're planning on making a beer run."

"Swing by on the way, room 316, and I'll go with y'all," Buck suggested.

"Will do," Ricky replied.

Buck backed the Chevelle out of the parking space and spun the tires as he turned onto Front Beach Road.

"The wild bunch is in town!" Ricky commented to no one, still amazed at the stolen Coke machine riding around in Jimmy's truck bed.

After three or four .38 Special songs, Jimmy appeared at Ricky's passenger side door.

"Alright," he said, climbing in the cab. "Let's roll."

"While you were inside," Ricky reported, "Buck showed up. Him and his brother have a room down at the Trade Winds. He said to swing by and get him on the way to buy beer."

"Sounds like a plan," Jimmy replied.

Ricky fired up the pickup, and they headed to get Buck.

When they arrived at the Trade Winds, Ricky surveyed the parking lot and picked out Buck's Chevelle parked in front of a block of rooms.

"Well," he stated, "he's around here somewhere."

Ricky parked the truck, and the two got out and approached the car. As they approached, Jimmy heard a sound and looked up at the balcony above him. He spotted Buck's little brother, Troy, carrying a duffle bag.

"I see his room," Jimmy said.

Ricky followed Jimmy up the stairs, and Jimmy knocked on the door of the room he had seen Buck's brother enter.

"Police. Search warrant. Open up!" he shouted as he knocked.

Buck threw the door open. "Funny. I don't imagine the cops sound that redneck when they knock." He laughed.

"I hear that the grocery store has the best price on beer here, so let's go," Jimmy recommended.

"Alright," Ricky replied.

Buck nodded. "My brother is headed down to the pool with some of his buddies, so we should be good. Let's roll."

They piled into Ricky's pickup and made their way to a nearby Kroger. As they cruised down the beer aisle, Ricky made a startling discovery.

"Hey, guys!" he called. "Check out this Cost Cutter beer." He pointed to yellow cans with the word "Beer" centered in bold black letters. At the top of each can was a dashed line and the image of a pair of scissors.

Jimmy and Buck turned their attention to Ricky.

"Reckon it's any good?" Jimmy asked.

"Well," Ricky continued, "it all tastes the same after six, right? And a case of this is a little less than a six-pack of Budweiser."

"I see where you're going with this," Jimmy replied.

Within several minutes, each of them had a case of Cost Cutter beer with a six-pack of their favorite brand sitting on top of it.

Amazingly, they all three checked out without being asked to provide proof of age. They slid their purchases in the back of Ricky's pickup and closed the tailgate. Ricky drove them back to the Trade Winds while carefully splitting his attention between the road and the girls in bikinis on the sidewalks.

Back at the Trade Winds, they carried their purchases up to Buck's room and filled their coolers from the hotel ice machine. Once done, they each carried a cooler down to the pool area and set up camp. Each poured a beer into a plastic Solo cup to remain as discreet as possible.

Around six that afternoon, they started to get hungry and considered their options. Ricky remembered seeing a Wendy's restaurant nearby.

"Anyone up for some slick and juicy hamburgers?" he asked with a grin.

"Sounds cheap enough for my budget," Buck responded.

Buck got his brother, and the four slid in the Chevelle and drove the short distance to the Wendy's. When they walked in, Ricky noticed a poster on the wall advertising what looked to him like a calf nursing bottle with a flexible straw in the center of the top. "Free With Any Large Fountain Drink," the poster said. He nudged Jimmy.

"Hey, y'all," he started. "Take a look at this handy jewel."

They both looked at the poster.

"OK," Buck said. "What about it? It looks like something to nurse a calf with."

Ricky grinned mischievously. "It's wrapped in that red foam to keep the drink cold, and the bottle isn't clear, so from the outside, you can't tell what someone is drinking. And it says it holds thirty-two ounces! That means it would amply handle two beers!"

Jimmy smiled. "And the law doesn't want open containers on the beach. Problem solved!"

The three ordered their meals with giveaway drink containers. Once done with dinner, they returned to the Trade Winds. Buck, Ricky, and Jimmy each filled their new drink jugs with two cans of their favorite brands of beer and headed for a walk down the beach.

Just after dark, someone sat out a portable stereo on a lounge chair on the beach behind the Holiday Inn, and soon a crowd congregated as if it were a low-budget bar. Buck, Ricky, and Jimmy promptly made their way in to the festivities. Around 1 a.m., they all had completely consumed their individual six-packs and were working their way through the Cost Cutter. Just before 2 a.m., they decided to pack it in for the night. Buck headed for his room at the Trade Winds, Jimmy elected to walk to his room just down the beach at Bikini Beach Resort, and Ricky drove back to his motel.

{ 12 }

Ricky woke around 8 a.m. to noise outside his hotel room door. His head ached from the previous night's cheap beer. He stepped in the bathroom to relieve himself and was startled at the green tint of his urine until it dawned on him that it was almost the same color as the Cost Cutter beer. He grabbed a Goody's Powder from his bag, dumped it in his mouth, and chased it with a big glass of water from the hotel sink.

"Blegh!" he exclaimed.

Nothing tasted much worse than Goody's Powder, but it sure worked well on hangovers. He peeled off his clothes from the night before and took a quick shower. He picked the bathing suit up from the floor and put it back on and grabbed a clean T-shirt from his bag, slid on his Converse, and headed back out the door. He remembered talking with Andy on the beach the night before. Andy had mentioned that he, Gil, and Ford had a room at the Holiday Inn with a kitchenette. He seemed to recall the room number, so he headed there in hopes of a free breakfast.

He parked the pickup and headed up the elevator to the fifth floor, made his way down to the room number he was pretty sure was theirs, and pounded on the door.

A bleary-eyed Andy opened the door.

"Morning there, sunshine," Ricky said. "Rough night?"

Andy nodded. "A couple beers too many maybe."

Ricky surveyed the room, which looked like it had been looted. "Did someone break in here last night?" he asked.

"Nah, we kinda crashed last night and our maid hasn't been through yet," Gil responded sheepishly.

Ricky chuckled.

Ford was in the kitchen wearing only a pair of underwear and digging through the refrigerator. "Well, let's see. We have six eggs, two hot dogs, two slices of bologna, three slices of ham, and a couple slices of pickle loaf. I guess we'll throw it all together and see what we got."

He cracked the eggs in a skillet and set it on a burner on the stove. He chopped up the assortment of luncheon meats and tossed them in the eggs and scrambled the concoction as it cooked. Soon he had a multicolored scrambled egg and something.

He called out to the rest of the guys in the room. "Alright, come and get it. Just don't look at it too hard or you might lose your appetite."

They fixed their plates and passed a jug of orange juice around among them. Each took a swig of orange juice straight from the jug.

"You're right," Andy piped up. "Ain't much to look at, but it's filling."

The rest of the guys laughed. Several winced from the twinge of pain in their heads from the laughter.

Ford looked up at Ricky. "You always were one to take a dare or a bet," he said.

"Yeah?" Ricky responded with a questioning tone.

"I got ten bucks that says you won't walk down the beach in your shorts, my cowboy boots, and Gil's cowboy hat with no shirt."

Ricky looked him in the eye. "Ten bucks, huh?"

Ford grinned. "Ten bucks."

"You're on!" Ricky replied, unable to pass on easy money.

He slipped on Ford's cowboy boots, which seemed a little narrow for his feet. Gil tossed him a straw cowboy hat. He slipped off his T-shirt and donned the cowboy hat.

"How do I look?" he asked with a grin.

"Like a redneck who has a farmer's tan," Ford replied pointing out his lily-white chest and brown neck and arms.

Everyone laughed.

"How far do I have to walk down the beach?" Ricky asked.

"To the Trade Winds and back," Ford answered.

Ricky made his way down to the beach and set off.

{ 13 }

Jimmy woke with cotton mouth and a bit of a headache. He rummaged around the room and through his bag and found a bottle of aspirin. He popped two in his mouth and swallowed them dry. He ran his fingers through his hair and staggered out on the balcony of his room. A little salt air and the sound of the ocean waves might ease the pounding in his temples.

He propped himself on the balcony railing, gazing out over the Gulf of Mexico, trying to gradually ease into the morning and the risen sun. Occasionally, he focused on some of the seagulls overhead as people began to appear on the beach. Some were out collecting seashells, others looking for lost items from the night before, and some out for a casual stroll.

As he glanced down the beach to his left, he could make out someone walking very deliberately through the sand. As the figure approached, it appeared he was struggling to maintain his footing in the loose sand. Jimmy instantly realized why. The approaching figure was walking on the beach in cowboy boots. He tried to adjust his eyes.

"What in the name of all that is holy?" he said out loud.

He refocused his eyes to realize it was Ricky—shorts, cowboy boots, hat, and no shirt. His arms were bronze, as were his neck and face, but his belly and legs were as white as a ghost.

Jimmy shivered from head to toe at the sight and walked back into his room and closed the door. He went to the bathroom sink and washed his face and beard with cold water. Despite his best efforts to wash the image of Ricky on the beach from his eyes, it seemed etched in his mind.

He sighed, opened the cooler, and popped the top on a can of beer.

"Maybe this will help," he said as he took the first long sip.

He looked around the room for something to eat. Near the TV sat the remains of a box of doughnuts from the day before. He flipped the top open to find one remaining doughnut. He picked it up and bit it in half.

"The breakfast of champions," he said. "Beer and day-old doughnuts."

Finishing the doughnut, he carried the beer into the bathroom and took a shower. He pulled on a pair of shorts and a T-shirt and headed downstairs to the pool with his cooler in tow.

When he reached the pool, Jimmy spotted Jenny and her two sisters lying on chaise lounges poolside. The lounger next to Jenny was unoccupied, with a towel draped over the back.

Jimmy greeted the girls as he approached. "Morning, ladies!"

Jenny rolled over onto her back to face him. He admired her formfitting one-piece bathing suit.

"Well good morning, cowboy," she said with a smile. "How ya feelin'?"

Jimmy grinned. "A little rough for the mileage, but I'll live."

She chuckled at his answer. "Got a little skint up last night did ya?"

Jimmy laughed. "Yeah, after I saw y'all. I met up with the guys and we drank a few till around one or something."

She shook her head playfully. "We were in bed around midnight. A gal's gotta get her beauty sleep."

Jimmy grinned. "Well, I'd say you have slept well," he said, and winked.

She pointed to the empty chair. "We saved you that one. Figured you'd eventually get out of the bed."

He sat his cooler down at the foot of the chair and dropped his frame onto the lounger.

"Reckon I could use a little tan," he joked.

One of Jenny's younger sisters threw a bottle of Coppertone toward Jimmy. "Better put on a little tan lotion there so ya don't fry."

Jimmy caught the bottle of suntan lotion one-handed. He pulled off his shirt and rubbed lotion across his chest, his legs, and finally the tops of his feet. He capped the bottle and tossed it back.

"Thanks. I love the smell of that stuff. The minute I smell it, I picture the beach. Even when I am just at the American Legion pool back home."

Jenny chuckled. "I call it the aroma of summer time."

Jimmy soon fell asleep in the sun.

After a couple of hours, he awoke to Jenny poking him in the ribs with a finger. "Ya got company. The wild bunch has arrived."

Jimmy rubbed his eyes and groggily sat up to see Ricky, Buck, and Troy strolling up. He noted Buck was carrying a couple buckets of Kentucky Fried Chicken.

"What's going on, guys?"

Buck grinned. "We brought lunch. Anyone hungry?"

Jimmy smiled. "Hell yeah."

Buck set the two buckets of chicken down. Troy set down a bag. "There's some bowls of mashed taters and gravy and some coleslaw in this bag and what not," he noted.

"What do we owe y'all?" Jenny asked.

"Nothn'!" Buck replied, feigning an innocent look. "We've been busy this morning."

Ricky laughed. "Damn right. Got up and got in the Chevelle and started riding the strip. Mustangs are a dime a dozen. And every one of them is driven by a kid that thinks he has the hottest car in town."

Jimmy smiled. "How many have you humiliated this morning?"

Without hesitation, Buck's little brother answered, "Six!"

Jimmy laughed. "I don't suppose you were giving them free lessons."

Buck chuckled. "Hell no! Fifty dollars a pop. So enjoy your free lunch. Compliments of the Chevelle. At this rate, I might take y'all out to one of the bars tonight, if we can manage to get everyone in."

"Oh Lord!" Jenny said between bites of chicken. "The wild bunch hits the bars of Panama City Beach—film at eleven. You got money for bail?"

"Aw," Buck responded, "we been up to the Midway Oyster Bar and the PII Club at home. We know how to behave in a bar."

"Uh huh," Jenny replied. "I'll pass on that and keep the girls entertained."

"Well, we can all do dinner at one of the seafood restaurants tonight, and then we can see what's happening," Jimmy recommended.

Jenny smiled. "Sounds like a plan. We'll do dinner with y'all, and then y'all can have boys' night."

{ 14 }

Around six o'clock, everyone piled into their cars and headed down to Capt. Anderson's. Jimmy ordered a Capt.'s Punch, Jenny ordered a frozen strawberry daiquiri, and Buck and Ricky ordered Rum Runners. When the waiter brought out their drinks in the signature hurricane glasses, everyone at the table wanted one. Luckily for Jenny's two sisters and Troy, they were able to order nonalcoholic drinks in hurricane glasses.

With the uproar over the signature souvenir hurricane glasses settled, everyone placed their orders for fresh seafood. Soon the table was covered in shrimp, oysters, crab cakes, scallops, and grouper.

Once the group finished dinner, they convened in the parking lot.

"Well," Jenny said, "these girls want airbrushed shirts, a walk on the beach, and the swimming pool. Y'all try not to get locked up. You know where to find us."

The guys laughed.

"How much trouble could we possibly get into?" Ricky asked innocently.

Allen Madding

Jenny laughed. "Not any more than usual, I suspect," she said pointedly, then gestured to Buck's little brother. "You better come with us." He nodded, hung his head in disappointment, and walked over to where her sisters were standing. The guys watched the girls drive off in Jenny's mom's station wagon.

"Where to, fellas?" Jimmy asked.

Ricky spoke up. "Andy and some of the guys suggested we meet them at the Crow's Nest on top of the Holiday Inn."

Jimmy shrugged. "Sounds as good as any, I guess."

They piled in Buck's Chevelle and drove to the Holiday Inn. Once up the elevator, they walked into the Crow's Nest and spotted Andy, Ford, and several other boys from home. They gathered at tables at one end of the room and ordered drinks. They laughed, drank, and made small talk for a few hours.

Suddenly, a panicked look crossed Ford's face. "Guys," he said, "take a nonchalant look towards the door. Three guys just walked in wearing dark suits and sunglasses."

"OK," Andy replied.

Gil spoke up. "OK nothing. It's dark outside. Sunglasses at night. Dark suits. That's ABC."

"ABC?" Andy questioned.

"Alcohol Beverage Control!" Jimmy answered.

"Shit!" Andy hissed as he surveyed the room for an alternative exit. "All I see is this fire escape exit," he said, pointing to a door behind Jimmy.

Well," Jimmy said calmly, "seeing only two of the six of us are legal, I suggest y'all casually ease out the fire exit. Ford and I will...parking lot."He looked over toward the suits and noted they were distracted talking to the bar manager near the door with their backs to the boys. "Nice and quiet, guys. Let's go," he commanded.

Ford and Jimmy moved to block the view of the fire exit while continuing to make small talk and enjoy their drinks.

Andy quietly made his way out the door. Methodically, the other three guys followed. Once out the door, they realized they were on the roof of the Holiday Inn. Ricky rapidly scanned the roof-top for a stairwell and noticed one on the other end of the long hotel roof.

"Alright guys, there's a stairwell way down that way," he said, pointing to the structure on the far end of the rooftop. "It's dark and there aren't any lights up here, so be careful. There will be roof vents, piping, and other obstacles. Don't bust your shins on something. We need to move fast, but don't run."

The four set off in the direction of the stairwell on the horizon. Ricky looked over his shoulder periodically as they made their way across the roof. Just as they reached the stairwell, he heard the fire exit door on the bar open, and he turned and saw light coming from the doorway.

"Hey! You over there! Stop!" a shadowy figure in the doorway hollered.

The guys scampered into the stairwell and out of sight.

Meantime, Ford and Jimmy paid the bar tab for the entire table and causally made their way to the front door. Just before they reached the door, one of the suits stepped in front of them.

"Excuse me, boys," the man said boldly. "Let's see some IDs."

Jimmy and Ford presented the man with their driver's licenses.

The man inspected them both and handed them back. "Alright. You're good," he said, sounding a bit dejected.

Out the corner of his eye, Jimmy could see another suit at the fire exit, looking out on the roof. He thought he heard the man shouting over the music in the bar, but he wasn't certain. Ford and Jimmy strolled out to the elevator and made their way to the parking lot.

Halfway down the five floors of stairs, a security guard stepped into Ricky and Andy's escape path.

"What are you fellas up to?" the security guard questioned.

"We were just leaving," Ricky said nervously.

"Y'all ain't causing no trouble, are ya?" the guard asked.

Ricky reluctantly dug a twenty-dollar bill out of his pants pocket, knowing it was their saving grace. He reached across the space between him and the security guard.

"Chief, we were leaving the rooftop bar. Not causing any trouble, but a couple of us might be a couple months short of drinking age," he explained.

The security guard grinned as he took the twenty-dollar bill.

"Alright fellas, get on your way before ABC comes snooping around here," he said, and he stepped out. The guys scrambled down the remaining stairs and into the parking lot. They used the cover of night and shadows to make their way across the parking lot, avoiding any outside lights until they met up with Jimmy and Ford.

"Y'all alright?" Jimmy inquired.

Ricky smiled. "Fine as frog hair, and I acquired a new friend— the night security guard."

Jimmy laughed. "Damned if you don't make friends everywhere you go!"

Andy and Ford headed to the hotel pool while Jimmy, Buck, and Ricky jumped in the Chevelle and headed for the Trade Winds.

{ 15 }

Thirty minutes later, Jimmy climbed the stairs off the beach leading to the pool area at the Bikini Beach Resort. His eyes scanned the deck and spotted Jenny and her sisters. He plopped down on a lounger next to Jenny.

"What's up, ladies?" he greeted them.

Jenny smiled. "Did y'all cut the night short?"

Jimmy smoothed his beard with his hand. "Seems the ABC guys did a little surprise visit to the Crow's Nest. A couple fellas were a few months short of the drinking age and were forced to beat a hasty retreat.

Jenny laughed. "No sweat off your back, you're legal."

"Right, right," Jimmy coolly replied. " 'cept my ride was two months shy. So once they got off the hotel roof, they figured they might ought to distance themselves from the property."

Jenny laughed again. "Probably not a bad idea," she said, rolling her eyes. "Up for a midnight stroll on the beach?"

Jimmy grinned. "You bet!"

"Girls," she said, turning to her sisters. "I'll see y'all back at the room later."

The two walked off into the night.

{ 16 }

Thursday afternoon, Jimmy was cruising the strip with Waylon Jennings's Greatest Hits playing in the truck's stereo while he sipped a beer. He casually glanced at the sights on both sides of the busy roadway as he drove. As he approached the small motel where Ricky was staying, something caught his eye. He decelerated and turned in to the cracked and patched parking lot to get a better look. As he approached, the image of Ricky standing over a large plastic trash can with a trolling motor clamped on the side came into clear view.

"What in the name of all that is holy and good are you doing?" Jimmy called to him as he stepped out of the truck.

Ricky laughed. "I'm making hunch punch! You can't have a beach trip without hunch punch!" he said as he wiped sweat off his brow.

Jimmy looked over into the trash can at what appeared to be around twenty-five to thirty gallons of liquid with cut-up oranges, pineapple, cherries, lemons, and limes floating on top.

"What all is in there?" he asked.

"Hawaiian Punch, Sprite, ginger ale, Everclear, Golden Grain, Jose Cuervo, Captain Morgan, and all the fresh fruit I could find," Ricky proudly reported while revving the trolling motor.

"Ain't that the Minn Kota off the front of your johnboat?" Jimmy asked, intrigued by what he was witnessing.

"One and the same!" Ricky replied.

"Did you wash the river water off of it before you stuck in this mix?" Jimmy probed further.

"What? You don't think this much alcohol won't sterilize it and kill any germs?" Ricky asked.

"Good point," Jimmy relented, knowing better than to enter the proverbial spiraling staircase into redneck logic.

Jimmy heard the deep rumble of a car pulling into the parking lot and momentarily diverted his attention from the swirling concoction to see Buck in his Chevelle.

"What the hell have you two got going on over here?" Buck inquired, stepping out of the Chevelle.

Jimmy shook his head. "Ricky's mixed up the largest quantity of hunch punch I believe I have ever witnessed. I've been from Maine to Spain, Austin to Boston, seen two World's Fairs, have balls big enough that they won't fit in a five-gallon bucket, and enough hair on my ass to weave two Indian blankets—"

Buck cut him off before he could finish his soliloquy. "And I ain't never seen something like this!"

All three of the guys broke into laughter. Buck looked at Ricky, who was still churning the mix with the trolling motor.

"That's a pretty high-dollar professional mixer you got there. I didn't know the grocery stores and liquor stores had started carrying Minn Kota," Buck said with a chuckle.

"He's starting a new trend," Jimmy joked. "All your bigger bars will be tossing out their blenders and buying Minn Kota trolling motors before the summer is over. Just wait and see."

"Where's Troy?" Jimmy asked Buck.

"Him and Jenny's sisters were headed to the miracle strip. They were wanting to look for airbrushed shirts and such," Buck explained.

Ricky reduced the power to the motor and shut it off. The contents of the barrel continued to swirl. He grabbed a Solo cup from a bag sitting on the sandy sidewalk near his feet and dipped it into the concoction. He took a big sip, smiled, and wiped his mouth on the sleeve of his T-shirt.

"I think it's right," he judged. "Who's up for the first round?"

Jimmy grabbed a cup from the bag.

"Hell, you only live once, right?" he said before dipping a cupful from the trash can. He took a long sip and smiled. "That's pretty tasty while packing a bit of a punch."

Buck followed suit and dipped himself a cup.

"Whew. It's got a little kick to it!" he reported after a big sip.

Ricky disconnected the trolling motor's power cable from his truck's battery and slammed the hood down. He unclamped the trolling motor from the trash can and carried it around to a beach towel spread out on the tailgate of the truck. When he turned to walk back to the trash can, he saw a station wagon pulling up.

"Y'all's girlfriend is here," he noted dryly.

Jenny swung open the door of the station wagon, staring at the three guys and the trash can with raised eyebrows. "Should I even ask?" she said with one hand on her hips.

"Hunch punch!" Ricky proudly announced.

"Oh hell," Jenny responded. "I've had Ricky's hunch punch before. This night isn't going to end well. Where's the cups?"

Jimmy laughed and tossed her a cup from the bag. She spotted a cooler, filled the cup with ice, and traded it to Jimmy for his now-empty cup, which she also filled with ice.

"Alrighty then," Jimmy said before dipping himself another cupful. He swirled the cup and took a sip—much more refreshing with the ice—as he stepped to the cab of his truck, turned the key, and flipped the radio back on.

Moments later, a white Mustang rolled up. Andy, Ford, and Gil popped out of the car.

"Is this where the party is happening?" Andy inquired.

"Apparently so," Jenny answered between sips from her cup.

Ford raised his eyebrows as he approached the garbage can. "Hunch punch, I presume?"

"Brilliant deduction, my dear Watson," Jimmy called to him.

"This is definitely where the party is then," Gil noted.

All three grabbed cups and filled them with ice and punch. Before long, other motor lodge guests—complete strangers—were gathered and drinking punch. Random people walking down the sidewalk soon joined the festivities.

After several rounds of punch, Jimmy climbed in the back of his truck, played air guitar, and sang with the truck's stereo to everyone's amusement.

Sometime after one in the morning—or maybe three—the trash can approached empty and the crowd dwindled. Andy, Ford, and

Gil elected to walk the few miles back to the Holiday Inn. Buck, Jimmy, and Jenny evaluated their options. They all three recognized they were too far into their cups to drive. After considering how long the walk was to Bikini Beach and the Trade Winds, they decided to pass on that strenuous exercise as well.

Jimmy assumed the role of spokesperson. "Hey, Ricky. Any chance you have enough room for us to pass out in your room?"

Ricky's eyes widened for a second. "Well, it's two full-size beds. So one of them is open."

"Hell, I'll just take lay on the floor," Buck offered.

Jimmy looked at Jenny. "Can you share a bed and behave?"

Ricky thought he noted Buck grimace at the prospect of Jimmy and Jenny sharing a bed, but apparently Buck's hunch punch consumption prevented him from protesting.

She snorted. "I ain't taking my clothes off. Just passing out, cowboy."

The four stepped in the small room and almost immediately passed out.

{ 17 }

Jenny woke to sun streaming through the tattered motel curtains directly into her face. She squinted as she attempted to open her eyes and focus—a dull ache in her head reminded her of the events of the last evening. She quickly took stock of the situation. Lying on top of the worn blanket, she was still wearing yesterday's clothes. She rolled over and poked Jimmy, who was snoring.

"Wake up," she commanded. "Apparently the world is alive outside." She grabbed the phone on the bedside table and dialed the number for her hotel room, which she'd scribbled on the back of a matchbook she had stuffed in her pocket.

As she was checking on her sisters at her hotel room, Jimmy opened one eye and grimaced. "Did you get the tag number of that truck?"

Ricky woke groggily and attempted to answer him. "What truck?"

"The one than ran through my head," Jimmy answered, rubbing his temples.

Ricky staggered from the bed to his feet and looked around the room. "Where the hell is Buck?" he asked.

Jenny looked over the edge of the bed where she was lying toward the bathroom. "Not over here," she reported.

Ricky staggered to the window and peered through the curtains. "Well, the Chevelle is still outside with the windows down."

Jimmy pushed his large frame to a standing position with some assistance from the sturdy nightstand between the two beds. He shuffled to the bathroom, pushed open the door, and announced, "Found him."

Buck was passed out in the bathtub, fully clothed.

Jimmy reached over the edge of the tub and poked him in the ribs. "You alive?"

Buck startled. "Jury's out. Either I am or I am in one of the levels of Dante's Inferno that has a big drum that someone won't quit pounding."

"Well, I hate to disturb your slumber, but I need to pee," Jimmy replied.

"Hold up. Hold up," Jenny interjected, lurching out of the bed. "Ladies first. Y'all clear out in there."

Jimmy reached down and hooked one of his large hands under Buck's shoulder and helped him out of the tub. The two staggered back into the room while Jenny hurriedly brushed past them, slamming the bathroom door behind her.

After everyone got through the bathroom, Buck dragged himself into the Chevelle and headed to his room. Jimmy and Jenny talked in hushed tones beside her mother's station wagon in the parking lot. Ricky was almost certain he saw them kiss before she rode off, leaving Jimmy looking a bit extra pleased.

"Well," Jimmy started, looking a bit extra pleased. "I guess I need to go get my stuff packed in the truck and checked out of the room."

Ricky nodded. "Hey, wanna go meet up at that all-you-can-eat pancake place after we have the trucks packed?"

"Sounds like a good idea. Maybe some pancakes and coffee will have us feeling a little more up for the drive home," Jimmy agreed.

Ricky showered, changed, and packed his clothes in his duffle bag, carefully wrapping his hurricane glass in a T-shirt and sandwiching it between some dirty clothes. Once he had everything loaded in the truck, he walked down to the office and gave the woman at the counter the key to his room.

"Hell of a party y'all threw last night," the woman noted. "But well behaved with no property damage." She slid a five-dollar bill across the counter to Ricky. "Key deposit refund," she explained. "Y'all be careful on your way home."

"Thanks," Ricky replied before walking back out to his truck.

Ricky spotted the breakfast restaurant at the base of a building that resembled a lighthouse. The sign in front advertised the local beach radio station and "All You Can Eat Pancakes $5." Ricky smiled as he considered the five bucks the motel clerk had just handed him.

He walked in and found a long table and plopped down in a chair. A waitress promptly greeted him.

"Expecting a crowd?" she asked.

"Well, kinda," Ricky answered. "The rest of the crew should be here shortly."

"Alright," she replied. "Coffee while you wait?"

"Please," Ricky responded.

She disappeared to the kitchen area. Buck and Troy walked through the glass door, scanned the tables, and made a beeline to Ricky.

"Jimmy said we'd find you here," Buck noted.

"Yeah," Ricky replied. "Maybe some pancakes and coffee will help lift my brain fog."

Buck chuckled. "Here's hoping."

The waitress returned with a carafe of coffee and two cups. She sat one on the table in front of Ricky and filled it.

"Either of you want coffee?" she asked, turning her gaze on Buck and his little brother.

"Yeah, I could use a cup," Buck replied somberly.

"I'll take an orange juice," Troy answered.

She sat a cup in front of Buck, who didn't look up from the table, and poured coffee as Jenny and her two sisters walked into the restaurant.

"There they are," Jenny said, pointing toward their table. As they sat down, Jimmy walked through the glass door.

"And the gang is all here," Ricky reported.

The waitress pulled a pad from her apron pocket and a pen from behind her ear and took all of their orders. She disappeared to the kitchen to hand off the orders and to fill drinks. Ricky noted Buck was unusually quiet, be it from nursing a hangover from the night before or his jealousy of Jimmy and Jenny sitting tight beside each other. Meanwhile Jenny's two sisters, sporting their new airbrushed T-shirts, were chattering away with Troy about their adventures at the Miracle Strip.

"You know, this is the part I always dread," Ricky commented, breaking the awkward silence among the older teenagers. "The four-hour drive home. It's just depressing. The drive down, you're all stoked up to be going to the beach, and you can't wait to get here. But the drive home just seems long and boring. It seems like you're heading the wrong direction because you're leaving the beach."

Jimmy nodded, taking a long sip of coffee from the mug the waitress had poured for him while Ricky was talking. "The party is over, and we return to our new daily lives. Now school's over. We now step into our new normal."

"What's your plan, Jimmy?" Ricky asked.

"I dunno," Jimmy answered. "I got a little side gig playing at the Midway Oyster Bar on Saturday nights starting next weekend. I talked to the manager at the parts house on Butcher County Road about a job. He said he'd let me know something next week or so."

Jimmy was interrupted as the waitress reappeared with a huge tray stacked with plates and passed them out. The table promptly became quiet as everyone was pouring syrup over stacks of pancakes with butter melting in the middle. As the group started devouring their food, the only sound was the clink of silverware against plates.

"I notice you're wearing a plain white T-shirt today, Ricky," Jenny said, breaking the silence.

"Yeah," Ricky replied with a mouthful of pancakes. He swallowed hard. "Trying to avoid any dyes in clothes irritating my sunburn. My chest and back are red as Buck's Chevelle. I slathered on Solarcaine, but geez Louise it still stings."

One of Jenny's sisters piped up, "Yeah, I fell asleep at the pool and burned my back and the back of my legs."

Jimmy nodded as he dove into his third plate of pancakes. "A sunburn is one of the traditional souvenirs from the beach."

Jenny laughed. "Yeah, reckon next time you'll remember to put sunscreen on your back?"

Jimmy nodded in agreement. "I reckon so!"

Once the crowd was sufficiently full, they paid the check and made their way to the parking lot.

"Well, I guess it's time to hit 231 for Dothan and through the woods to Butcher County and home," Jimmy said. "Y'all gonna be uptown tonight?"

"We'll see how I feel once I get home and unpacked. This sunburn is tough," Ricky answered. He looked at Buck, who'd seemed silent and distant all the way through breakfast. "What about it, Buck?" "Yeah, prolly," he replied curtly.

"Alright, I'll see y'all at the OK Corral," Jimmy said as he slammed the door on his pickup and cranked the engine.

"Y'all drive safe," Jenny called out as she and her sisters loaded into the station wagon.

{ 18 }

A round 7 p.m., Jimmy rode into town. He took a lap and noted several kids had made it back from the beach. He saw some still sporting their airbrushed T-shirts and sunburns.

He turned onto Broad Street and into the city parking lot. He parked his truck across a couple parking spots facing the street and popped the top on a beer. He sat watching the slow parade of cars circle through the parking lot and back out, making the lap through town and out to US 19. Andy, Gil, and Ford rode through in Andy's Mustang, and Andy threw up a one-finger wave, and Jimmy cheerfully returned the gesture.

After an hour or so, Jenny pulled into the parking lot and pulled driver's side to driver's side with Jimmy's truck, allowing them to chat without getting out of their cars.

"Ya'll got home alright, I see," Jimmy noted.

"Yeah," Jenny replied, "pretty uneventful trip. Both of the girls fell asleep before we were out of Florida. They both went to bed after dinner."

Jimmy chuckled. "Between the sunburn and the late nights, I'm sure they were both pretty worn out." Without pause, he dove into the thought that had been nagging at him since breakfast: "Hey, any idea what's up with Buck? He seemed kinda removed from the gang this morning."

Jenny nodded. "I told him I had decided I wanted to date you exclusively in the parking lot before breakfast. He didn't seem to take it too well. He was polite and all, but you could tell he didn't like my decision."

"Ah!" Jimmy said, stroking his beard with one hand. "That 'splains it. I guess I am the enemy for a while." While pleased that Jenny had chosen to go steady with him, Jimmy hated that it would damage his friendship with Buck, at least temporarily. He hated drama, and he was slap dab in the middle of it.

"Surely he wouldn't let this come between y'all's friendship," Jenny exclaimed.

"I don't know if it will or not, and stop calling me Shirley," Jimmy joked.

"I hope y'all are bigger boys than that," Jenny continued, ignoring the joke. Her squinted eyes revealed a level of concern for the negative impact of her decision.

"Aw," Jimmy said. "We've been buddies since middle school. He'll get over it. Just give him some time and space. Hell, Haggard is a small town. It's not like you can hide out with another set of friends in another area of town." As he spoke, Jimmy internally questioned his own words. He wondered how long Buck would sulk and if at some point they'd be able to hunt and fish together again.

"True," Jenny replied.

"Well, to the victor goes the spoils," Jimmy announced. "Why don't you crawl in and ride with me for a bit."

"Alright," Jenny answered. She squirmed into the passenger side of the truck and slid to the center of the bench seat. She turned and gave Jimmy a peck, and they set off to ride dirt roads outside of town.

After a couple hours of riding random dirt roads, they made a lap through town. Jimmy saw Buck's Chevelle and Red's Mustang sitting at the far end of the city parking lot when they came through. When he glanced that direction, he saw Buck turn and look their way and briskly divert his eyes to the ground. Buck spun around to face away from them. Disappointed, Jimmy quietly continued back out onto Broad Street and then Main Street towards the highway.

"Well," Jimmy said dryly, breaking the silence. "I guess that confirms that he's still pissed with the two of us."

"Small-town drama," Jenny bemoaned dismissively. "I just wanna be happy!" she pleaded, trying to justify the situation to herself. "And I am always happy with you," she followed, looking for affirmation from Jimmy.

Just before midnight, Jimmy drove back into the city parking lot, pulled up to Jenny's mom's station wagon, and shut off his truck. He glanced to the far end of the parking lot at the edge of the alley and noticed Buck's Chevelle backed into a corner parking spot. He opened Jenny's car door for her, and she stopped and gave him a kiss before sliding into the driver's seat.

"See ya tomorrow, cowboy. Sweet dreams," she said.

"Goodnight, darlin'," he replied.

As she closed the driver's door and started the station wagon, Jimmy heard the Chevelle's engine fire up. His head jerked to look that direction. A loud metallic clank resounded as the Chevelle was slammed into gear, followed by the loud squall of spinning tires as it hooked sideways into the alley, disappearing out of sight.

He shook his head and quietly walked back to his truck.

{ 19 }

Jimmy drove through town toward Jenny's house Saturday evening and noticed a lot more kids riding around town. He figured a lot of them had gotten home late Friday and were too tired from the week at the beach and the long drive home to consider riding around Friday night. But now they had all rested up and were itching to get out and hang out with their friends.

Jimmy briefly chatted with Jenny's mother in the kitchen before Jenny came in from the back of the house.

"Y'all stay out of trouble, and try to have her home before sunrise," her mother chided. "I expect her to be in church in the morning."

"Yes, ma'am," Jimmy responded. He opened the door to the carport and escorted Jenny to his pickup.

"Wanna go to Pizza Hut for dinner?" he asked.

"Sure, it's either that or Dairy Queen," she commented, naming the only other restaurant open on Saturday nights.

When they arrived at the Pizza Hut, there was a pretty good crowd, but nothing compared to a Saturday night after a football game. They made their way to Jimmy's favorite booth in the corner of the restaurant.

"Let me guess," Jenny said. "You like this because you aren't close to the door, but you have clear view of the door, and no one can come up from behind you."

Jimmy nodded. "And I have a clear view of the parking lot, so I can see who's cruising town as they make their lap through the parking lot. And because they have to brake to make the turn in the parking lot at the corner of the building, I can even tell who is riding with who."

"Riding with whom," Jenny mischievously corrected.

Jimmy raised one eyebrow. "Touché," he responded, conceding the point.

They ordered a pizza and drinks and made small talk while they waited for their food. Jimmy glanced out the corner window as they talked and noticed Buck's Chevelle come by a couple of times in the steady stream of cruisers riding through the parking lot on their laps around town.

On one of the passes, Jenny noticed the Chevelle.

"I hope he gets over this whole hurt puppy thing that he has going on. I was forced to decide between the two of you. He had to have at least considered that this was a possibility," she said, stirring her drink with a straw.

"I'm sure in the back of his mind he knew it was a possibility, but he wouldn't have wanted to admit it even to himself. A guy never likes to consider he could lose at something. I mean, look at Buck. A large chunk of his ego rides on winning every weekend racing the Chevelle. Hell, I bet he left Panama City Beach with over a thousand dollars from street racing. In fact, I'm pretty sure he came home from the beach with more money than he left with. Tell me how many times anyone has done that! So after whipping everyone's tail drag racing, he begins to feel invincible. And then, he loses out in the final decision in a love triangle."

Jenny took a long sip of her drink. "You guys and your egos. Geez," she said with a distinct bit of disgust in her voice.

Jimmy dismissed her disapproval with a quick arch of his eyebrows and a shrug of his shoulders.

After they finished dinner, they rode into town and turned in to the city parking lot. Jimmy stopped in his normal spot and Ricky pulled up alongside.

Jimmy looked over and was a bit surprised to see the blonde gymnast that Ricky had been eyeing for a long time was now sitting on the passenger side of his truck.

"Hi, Mary!" Jenny called out as she and Jimmy exited the truck and each took a position on opposite sides of Ricky's truck.

"Hey, Jenny, how y'all?" Mary responded.

Ricky and Jimmy looked at the girls starting to chat and then back at each other, a bit dumfounded. They scrambled to regain their wits and chatted while the girls compared their week at the beach.

As they talked, Jimmy noticed the Chevelle turn in the parking lot and stop a noticeable distance from where they sat. He thought to himself that it was a sign of improvement over the previous night, when Buck sat at the far end of the parking lot at the edge of the alley.

As they chatted, Jimmy saw Troy get out and walk over to a car with some girls from school to talk. But Buck remained seated in the car. Meanwhile a parade of cars continued to snake through the parking lot and back out onto Broad Street, making another lap. He saw Andy pull up and stop near Buck's Chevelle. Andy, Gil, and Ford emerged from the car. Buck climbed out of the Chevelle and made small talk with them. Jimmy noted that Buck seemed a little unsteady on his feet.

Jimmy and Ricky continued talking about fishing, the farm, their plans for the remainder of the summer, and the like while the two girls were still chatting. Everyone seemed to be having a good time. As the night wore on, more cars stopped near where they sat, and more kids joined the small crowd chatting near their cars. Jimmy, Ricky, and the girls eventually meandered from the cabs of the trucks to chat with others in the crowd and empty a few beer cans.

Eventually, Troy made his way through the crowd to where Ricky and Jimmy were sitting on their tailgates.

"Would y'all mind keeping an eye on Buck tonight?" he requested somewhat sheepishly.

"Sure," Ricky responded, always ready to help a friend. "What's up?"

Troy looked from side to side quickly to make sure he wasn't overheard. "He's been drinking since like ten this morning. Really unusual for him. He usually doesn't pop the first top until after dinner as he's riding up here. He's pretty tore up about Jenny and all. I don't want him to get in a wreck or something, and heck, I gotta ride home with him."

Jimmy frowned at the news and quietly shook his head in disappointment.

"We gotcha," Ricky replied without a second thought.

Jimmy watched as Ricky stood from the tailgate, tossed his empty beer can into the bed of his truck, and walked over to the

Chevelle, where Buck sat slumped over in the center of the front seat.

"How's it going, Buck?" Ricky greeted him.

"Ah, alright I guess," Buck responded, his words slightly slurred. "I whipped a couple out-of-towners earlier that thought they were hot shit in a Pinto."

Ricky laughed. "I can't figure how anyone driving a Pinto would think they could outrun the Chevelle."

Buck laughed, sloshing some of his open beer onto his pants. "They were so sure that they lost seventy-five bucks!" he said, slurring again.

Ricky became more concerned the more he listened to Buck and watched him spilling his beer. He eyed the keys in the Chevelle's ignition as Buck continued to talk. When he saw an opening, he quickly reached in the open driver's window and pulled the keys out.

"Hey! Hey! What the hell do you think you're doing?" Buck shouted, trying to right himself in the seat, struggling to open the driver's door, and then finally scrambling out of the car.

Everyone in the crowd immediately turned around to see what the commotion was. Jimmy jumped to his feet and sprinted to the Chevelle, stopping in front of the driver's side fender.

Buck continued shouting, "Give me my damn keys!"

Ricky held one hand up. "Buck, you've had too much to drink to be driving. Just simmer down. We'll get you home when you're ready to leave, but I don't want you getting in a wreck or something."

"Give me my damn keys," Buck demanded. "I'm fine. I don't need you to lecture me on drinking. I've seen you drunk before too, mister!"

He darted toward Ricky.

Ricky continued, trying to persuade him. "Buck, just calm down. We'll take you anywhere you wanna go. I just don't want you driving."

Buck slung a fist and hit Ricky across the bridge of his nose and blood flew.

"Dammit, Buck!" he shouted, throwing a hand to his face as pain shot across both of his cheekbones.

Not wanting to see trouble between friends, and feeling partly to blame for the altercation, Jimmy jumped between them to defuse the situation.

"Give him his keys," Jimmy commanded. "I'll stay with him."

Ricky shrugged, still holding his face, and tossed the keys to Jimmy. "You give 'em to him. I'm not gonna be responsible for him."

Jimmy caught the keys midair. Buck turned toward him, and Jimmy held them out to him.

Buck snatched the keys out of Jimmy's hand. "Screw both of y'all. Ruining my night and ruining my life. Stole my girl and trying to steal my car."

He staggered back to the driver's side of the car, clambered under the steering wheel, and slammed the long driver's door.

{ 20 }

As Buck started the car, Ricky jumped back from where he was standing to ensure he didn't get run over. Jimmy ran to the passenger side, flung the door open, and jumped in the car. Buck slammed the Chevelle into gear and spun tires, heading out onto Broad Street.

"Slow down and calm down," Jimmy shouted, loud enough that everyone in the parking lot could hear him over the car.

As they squealed out of the parking lot, Jenny and Mary ran to Ricky.

"Are you OK?" Mary asked.

"I think the damn fool broke my nose," Ricky answered.

Jenny handed him a wad of paper napkins from the door pocket of Jimmy's truck to help him stop the bleeding.

Troy ran over to check on him. "I'm sorry, Ricky. I didn't mean to get you hit. I just didn't want him to do anything stupid."

"It's alright," Ricky assured him. "I've had worse."

"I hope Jimmy can calm him down before he does something stupid," Jenny said.

"If anyone can talk sense into him right now, it would be Jimmy," Ricky responded. "They've hunted and fished together since grade school." Despite the pit in his stomach, Ricky hoped that Jimmy could get through to Buck before things got worse.

With the shouting and tire squealing over, the crowd resumed their conversations, and the parade of cars continued to cruise through the parking lot. Thirty minutes later, the crowd's conversations were interrupted by sirens. The only two city police cars flew past the parking lot with blue lights flashing and sirens wailing. They heard another long siren as the ambulance raced by.

Ricky's heart sank. He tossed the bloody napkin, and swore under his breath. He saw the color drain from Jenny's face. Ricky jumped into his pickup and fired up the engine. Mary climbed in from the passenger side and slid across to the middle of the bench seat, and Jenny jumped in behind her, slamming the truck door. Ricky took off in the direction the police cars and ambulance had headed. Maintaining enough presence of mind to watch his speed, Ricky was glad he hadn't had too much beer as he controlled the desire to rush but needed to avoid another disaster.

Just south of town on highway, they spotted the police cars stopped at the intersection of the road going to the city football stadium. Ricky turned up the road and pulled off on the opposite shoulder, allowing the police and ambulance plenty of room. He scrambled out of the truck, across the road, and to the edge of what he estimated to be a thirty-foot-deep ditch. When he looked over, he could see Buck's Chevelle lying upside down on its crumpled roof. He glanced toward the ambulance and could see the EMTs retrieving equipment.

Ricky ran down into the deep ditch, sliding and stumbling on the way. He could feel blackberry stickers tearing at his arms and hands. When he reached the car, Buck had already wiggled out and was struggling to stand up with the assistance of one of the cops. Ricky dove down to the passenger window.

"Jimmy!" he shouted.

"Damn it!" Jimmy screamed in pain. "I can't get out. Get my shotgun out of my truck and shoot me!"

"Calm down!" Ricky ordered. "We'll get you out of here."

"Please!" Jimmy bellowed. "Ricky, just get my shotgun and shoot me in the head. I can't take this!"

The two EMTs descended on the car as the two cops grabbed Buck and wrestled him up the hill.

Ricky looked up at the EMTs. "He's trapped!" he screamed.

One of the EMTs hollered up at a city cop. "Get us a tow truck; we need some help getting him out."

The other EMT climbed through the driver's side of the car to attend to Jimmy and assess his situation. The first EMT returned to the car on the side where Ricky was frantically snatching on the crumpled passenger door.

"The front of the car is pushed back enough it's got the door jammed, and the firewall and dash are crushed down on his legs," Ricky pointed out. "If we could get this damn door open, we could try and make him some room."

Jimmy continued to moan in pain. Ricky suspected that he probably had two broken legs if not worse. The EMT inside the car was assessing Jimmy's injuries and calling out vital signs to the one that was attempting to help Ricky free his friend from the overturned car.

As he continued to snatch on the door, he thought he could smell gasoline leaking from the tank.

"We gotta get him out of here!" Ricky shouted at the EMT. "I can smell a gasoline leak."

Frustrated with the lack of progress being made by the EMTs, Ricky ran back up the hill to where his truck was parked. He reached under the seat and pulled out a long crowbar and ran back across the road and down into the ditch, again stumbling and sliding on the way down. When he reached the car, the EMT had another crowbar and was trying to pry the door open.

Together with two bars, they managed to break the door open at the latch, but it was so bent it would not fully open. Ricky shoved his back into the car, placed a cowboy boot against the door, and started kicking with all of his might. As he worked, he noted Jimmy's moans were fading, and he began to worry that they might be losing him. He had enough adrenaline worked up that he finally kicked the door completely open and then some, breaking the hinges so it bent back more than its usual ninety degrees. "We need a backboard and a C-collar," the first EMT hollered up to the crowd forming at the street above them.

Ricky pointed to the seat. "If we can break that seat back, we can slide him up and out of there," he suggested.

The EMT shined a flashlight into the area where Jimmy's legs were pinned, and to the seat hanging upside down.

"I think you may be right," he noted, then screamed toward the road above, "Someone get us a hacksaw!"

A city cop scrambled down the side of the ditch with a back-board and a foam collar.

"This seat has a latch to hinge forward to get in the back seat since it's a two-door," Ricky noted. "I bet we can break that and make it fold back."

Someone scrambled down to the car with a hacksaw. Ricky grabbed it and sawed at the base of the seat. It quickly gave way due to the damage it had sustained in the wreck. He gave it a couple hard shoves, and the back of the seat flopped backwards. Jimmy moaned as the seat moved and his body shifted. One EMT struggled to provide Jimmy support as Ricky removed the obstacles.

"I think we could carefully lift him out of there," the EMT reported, shining the flashlight down on Jimmy's legs.

Two city cops and the other EMT climbed in and gently lifted Jimmy out of the car and onto a wooden backboard. Ricky scrambled out of the way as they prepared to move him.

Jimmy screamed in agony as they moved him. Ricky flinched in empathy, Jimmy's earlier request still echoing in his mind. Once they had him completely on the board, they fastened what looked like seatbelt straps around him to hold him on the board. One of the EMTs secured the foam collar around his neck, and the five of them ascended the hill to carry him up to the road above.

When they reached the road, they laid the board with Jimmy strapped to it on the grass shoulder, and one of the EMTs worked to stabilize Jimmy's legs. The other jogged to the ambulance for the stretcher, grabbing a cop to help on the way. Ricky looked up to see Buck in handcuffs, standing at the rear of one of the cop cars. Ricky could see a lump on his forehead and a few scratches on his arms.

"Damned fool," Ricky muttered to himself.

They lifted the backboard with Jimmy onto the stretcher, secured some more straps, and loaded him into the ambulance.

"We're going straight to Dolor to the regional hospital," the EMT told Ricky as he closed the rear doors of the ambulance.

Ricky asked the cops to go wake Jimmy's parents and tell them to meet the ambulance at Dolor Regional Emergency Room. He headed to the truck and the girls.

Allen Madding

{ 21 }

James Sr. burst through the doors of the emergency waiting room and headed straight for Ricky. his face was crimson red, and the veins in his forehead were bulging.

"This is all your fault!" James Sr. bellowed, standing inches from Ricky's face.

"How you figure?" Ricky asked with a look of confusion, stepping back from the man. Ricky could feel the muscles in his right arm tighten and twitch as he struggled to repress his desire to punch James Sr. square in his face.

"If you were any kind of friend, you wouldn't have let Buck drive. You should've took his keys," James Sr. snorted.

"He did," Jenny interjected. "Buck got so mad he broke Ricky's nose for it."

"Yeah. And for the record, I didn't give him his keys back. I gave them to Jimmy. Jimmy gave Buck his keys and crawled in the car with him," Ricky explained.

"Well, you still should have stopped it. I hold you responsible," James Sr. continued.

Ricky threw up his hands and shook his head. "No one could ever talk any sense to you anyhow."

"What's that supposed to mean?" James Sr. asked.

Jimmy's mother stepped between them, displaying skills learned from being married to James Sr. for twenty-five years and having to defuse his explosive and illogical temperament. Her eyes, swollen from crying, and her disheveled appearance hinted that she had been in a rush getting dressed. "James, this isn't going to solve anything," she said.

A doctor with a grave expression on his face walked into the waiting area and approached them.

"Are you Jimmy Lowe's parents?" he asked.

"Yes," Jimmy's mother answered.

"He's in pretty rough shape. He has a shattered hip, a broken femur, two broken ribs, and a punctured lung. We have stabilized him and are preparing him for surgery. If you'd like to see him before we send him up to the surgery suite, we have a few minutes," the doctor explained.

Ricky was still shaking with adrenaline from his confrontation with James Sr. He sat down and stared at the clock on the wall. He felt overwhelmed with frustration from his failed attempt to prevent Buck from drunk driving and Jimmy's resulting serious injuries. Worse, he was taking the blame for it from James Sr.

Jimmy's parents followed the doctor through a set of doors leading to the emergency room. This left just Ricky, Jenny, and a handful of waiting patients; they'd dropped Mary off at home on their way to the hospital.

Remarkably composed despite the evening's events, Jenny walked to the emergency room reception counter. "I have a guy out here that needs to be looked at. I believe he has a broken nose and a few minor abrasions."

Realizing she was talking about him, Ricky looked down at his arms, which had several cuts from the blackberry vines and from the jagged metal on the remains of Buck's car.

After several minutes, a nurse called him to the counter area and took his information. She led him to an exam room. The ER staff cleaned the cuts on his arms and performed an X-ray of his face, confirming his nose was broken. A doctor set his nose and taped it in place. A nurse gave him an ice pack.

"I suggest you keep this on your nose to control as much of the swelling as you can. Both of your eyes are turning black. Whatever hit you did a hell of a job."

Ricky nodded. "Yeah. I'd say."

After signing some paperwork, Ricky returned to the waiting room to find only Jenny remaining from the original crowd.

"We're headed up to the surgery waiting area," Jenny called to him. "Come on."

"I don't think James Sr. wants me around," Ricky replied, wanting to get away by himself to process his thoughts. "I think I'll head home."

"Suit yourself," Jenny replied. She turned and headed for the elevators.

Ricky headed for the parking lot.

{ 22 }

Lying flat on his back in the hospital bed, Jimmy stared at the dark ceiling of his hospital room. The meds he had been given had significantly reduced the level of pain he was experiencing, allowing him to think through the events of the last several hours. Preferring to be in charge of matters, he had always insisted on driving his truck wherever he went. Rarely had he been one to ride in anyone else's car, and now that had gotten him in this situation. He glanced down his abdomen, dimly lit by light from the equipment sitting next to the bed. His hospital gown showed the outlines of the pins sticking out of his hips, and one of his legs was in traction.

"Damn it, Buck!" he thought to himself. "I shoulda just driven him home."

But Jimmy knew that Buck didn't let anyone else drive the Chevelle. And with Buck already fuming from his showdown with Ricky, Jimmy hadn't wanted to get Buck riled up any more than he already was. In an attempt to calm him, Jimmy had made the hasty choice to jump in the passenger seat—a move he would live to regret.

He looked up at the handle over his chest, suspended by chain from the frame of the bed. He grimaced. Nine weeks—that's what the doctor had told him. Nine weeks of lying flat on his back, using a bedpan, unable to move or walk. What on earth would he do for nine weeks lying in a hospital bed? This was going to screw up his plans. He had lined up a couple local gigs playing guitar and thought it might be the start of a possible career in country music. That dream was over.

Then there was his father. He hadn't heard it yet, but he knew shortly he would get a dressing down from James Sr. If nothing else, his father could be counted on for a good ass chewing, deserved or not. In eighteen years, Jimmy couldn't remember a single time when the old man had said "good job" or told him that he was proud of him. But he had a vivid memory of his fault findings and harsh disapprovals. He had been anxious to get a job and get out of his father's house. He couldn't get out on his own fast enough. Now this was going to delay that, and worse, he was certain he would have to recover at home.

Jenny—he smiled for the first time in several hours. She reminded him somewhat of his mom—calm, level headed, and in charge. She had stayed at the hospital until he had come out of surgery and moved to this room. He could still smell her perfume and feel the warm, wet kiss she had planted on his forehead before she went home.

The sharp pains in his hips and ribs were beginning to intensify again. He closed his eyes and tried to sleep.

{ 23 }

When Ricky awoke Sunday morning, the pain in his face had increased. He inspected the damage in the bathroom mirror to find two black eyes and a swollen nose.

"Perfect," he said with sarcasm dripping from the corners of his mouth.

He walked to the kitchen, where both of his parents were sitting at the table. Ricky retrieved one of the bags of frozen peas from the freezer and placed it across the bridge of his nose. His winced at the freezing temperature against the skin of his face. His mother quietly picked up a dish towel, took the bag of peas from him, wrapped them in the towel, and gently laid the make-shift ice pack back across his face.

"Thanks, Mom," he said.

His dad looked up from a cup of coffee. "Damn, son, he did that with one punch? You look like a bad stretch of Georgia asphalt."

"Yeah," Ricky replied. "And to top it off, James Sr. says it's my fault for not stopping him."

"Bullshit," his dad replied.

Ricky was stunned to hear his father curse. He couldn't remember ever hearing him use profanity.

"That man doesn't want to sling those kinda unfounded accusations in my presence. I'll give him a little taste of what Buck gave you."

Ricky forced a shrug. "It was all I could do not to punch him in the throat when he said it. Jimmy insisted I give him Buck's keys, and Jimmy gave 'em back to him. If he wants to be pissed at someone, he can take that up with Jimmy. Kinda ironic. I tried to prevent the whole thing. Then when it all went bad, I'm down in that ditch with my nose bleeding, working to get Jimmy out of the wreckage. His ol' man is an ungrateful son of a..."

Ricky's dad held up his hand. "Easy there, son."

Ricky nodded. He began to eat breakfast, but was distracted as he churned the events of the previous night over in his head. As his anger eased, he thought about how the EMTs didn't seem prepared for dealing with a vehicle damaged that severely.

"Pop. How old do you have to be to volunteer with the county fire department?"

His dad looked up from his coffee. "I believe to get your state certification as a firefighter, ya have to be eighteen. Are ya thinking of volunteering?"

Ricky laid his fork down on his plate. "Well, I've been thinking since everything last night. Maybe I ought to get involved. I know a lot about vehicles. I can drive everything we own out here, including the two-and-a-half-ton flatbed truck."

His dad nodded. "Well, why don't you ride up to the station Tuesday night. They have a meeting every week. I'm sure they could use some more help maintaining equipment. Chief Wilson can answer your questions about training and such."

Ricky's mom looked over the top of her reading glasses.

"Now quit playing with your food and eat."

Ricky glanced up at her. "Yes, ma'am."

He picked up his fork and started eating.

"If you wanna skip church with us this morning and ride up to Dolor to the hospital to see Jimmy, we're good with it," she said after waiting for him to eat a few bites.

Ricky looked up from his plate.

"Thanks. I guess I should. His ol' man better hold his tongue. I'm not in the mood for any more of his abuse."

Ricky's dad nodded. "If he starts up again, set him straight. Try to be respectful, but don't pull any punches."

After fifteen minutes or so, Ricky dropped his fork in the plate of half-eaten breakfast. He tossed the bag of frozen peas he had been balancing on his nose back in the freezer and headed for his truck.

{ 24 }

When Ricky walked into Jimmy's hospital room, he was surprised by what looked like monkey bars clamped to the bed over Jimmy. A quick glance around the room revealed Jimmy's parents were nowhere in sight.

"What's up, redneck?" Jimmy called out to him stoically. He was lying flat on his back with one leg in traction and the sheet elevated across his waist.

"You look as rough as a corncob there, bud," Ricky noted.

"You don't look too sporty yourself. Hey, I got the doc to write a prescription for a beer a day while I am in here. There is a cooler there at the foot of the bed if you want one," Jimmy said.

"Seriously? You have a beer cooler in the hospital?" Ricky asked, shaking his head in disbelief.

"Yeah. I refused morphine, and he wanted to give me something for pain. I told him I would take a beer." Jimmy grinned. "They originally gave me morphine in the ER, and I didn't like how it made me feel—sweating, stomach cramps. I talked them down to Tylenol #3 or beer. I can't have 'em together, so I got options."

"How long they thinking you're gonna be in here?" Ricky asked.

"Doc says prolly nine weeks, depending on how my pelvis heals," Jimmy replied, carefully pulling back the sheet to reveal eight long stainless-steel pins sticking up from his pelvis. "They got all this hardware holding me together at the moment. I feel like someone lost an erector set at some point last night."

"I'd say," Ricky replied. "That some impressive stuff. Do you get to keep them after they take them out?"

"I sure hope so!" Jimmy chuckled and winced from the pain in his ribs. "So I suddenly have a lot of time on my hands. Can you find me some reading material? A Hot Rod magazine, fishing magazines, maybe even some long books of some sort? I can't lay here and watch TV for nine weeks."

"Yeah. I'll see what I can do," Ricky answered.

"Thanks. Oh! By the way. About five this morning, me and the ol' man had a little shouting match. After I got over the anesthesia, Jenny told me about his temper tantrum in the ER waiting room. He came waltzing in here a few minutes later, and I laid into him. Mom was trying to calm me down, but I gave him both barrels. Hell, I gave Buck his keys and jumped in the car with him. He can't blame anyone but me. Heck, you got a swollen face trying to keep him from driving. And after all the work you did to get me out of the wreck, I think he not only owes you an apology but a huge thank-you. Of course, I doubt he'll ever be man enough to do either, because he can't admit he was wrong. But, thanks for getting me out of that mess. Seemed like the cops and all were hem-hawing trying to figure out what to do."

Ricky nodded. "Ain't nothing you wouldna done if it had of been one of us."

Ricky heard a noise and turned to see Buck and his dad at the door. Buck was holding his baseball cap in his hands. Ricky could feel his right arm muscles tighten and his pulse quicken. He struggled to restrain himself at the sight of Buck. "I think I am gonna go downstairs to see if I can find you some reading material. You have some company to see you," Ricky said.

Jimmy turned his head toward the door. "Come on in."

Ricky glared at Buck as he walked past him.

"You got one coming, ol' boy," Ricky said.

Buck swiftly diverted his eyes to the floor.

Allen Madding

{ 25 }

When Ricky returned to Jimmy's hospital room, Buck and his dad were gone. Ricky spread the results of his shopping trip across the table sitting beside the bed.

"Here is a copy of Motor Trend, Hot Rod, Car and Driver, Popular Mechanics, Popular Science, Outdoor Life, American Hunter, Fresh Water Fisherman, and the first book in a series of sci-fi books that came highly recommended—Dune."

Surprised by the amount of reading material and wondering where Ricky came up with the money to buy it all, Jimmy chuckled. "Well, that ought to keep me busy for a bit."

Ricky nodded. "So what did Buck have to say for himself?"

"He apologized," Jimmy stated dryly. Ricky thought he detected disappointment as he continued. "The city police wrote him a ticket for reckless driving, and his granddad is giving him his '72 pickup."

Ricky couldn't believe his ears. "So he will be back to driving tomorrow, and you're in traction for two months. That's screwed up."

Jimmy shrugged. "Life isn't always fair," he noted.

"Well, he's still got a butt whipping coming from me for the cheap shot when I took his keys away and for what he's done to you," Ricky replied.

"Come on, Ricky. He didn't mean to crash the car. It was an accident. I should've known better than to have crawled in that car, but I felt kinda responsible with the whole thing over Jenny. I knew if I tried to insist on driving his Chevelle, he would have wanted to fight me. I just wanted to defuse the whole thing."

Ricky shook his head. "It was a preventable accident. He was throwing a temper tantrum because Jenny picked you over him. And in the end, he's responsible for his actions."

Jimmy nodded. "Can't argue there."

Saturday, April 23, 1983

Allen Madding

{26 }

Ricky stood next to Jimmy at the front of the First United Methodist Church. Jimmy was wearing a black tuxedo and black cowboy boots and propping himself up with a cane. Jenny's mother and grandmother along with her sisters had worked overtime in the flower shop. The sanctuary showed it, as it was brimming with flower arrangements.

It seemed to Ricky that half the county had turned out for the wedding as there was hardly an empty seat to be found.

Jimmy beamed with pride as he watched Jenny being escorted down the aisle. Ricky stood silently by his side, watching him struggle to remain standing for the lengthy service.

When the ceremony concluded, Jimmy raised Jenny's veil and kissed his bride. Together they gradually descended the platform to the aisle and proceeded to the rear of the sanctuary. Even after almost a year of therapy and operations, Ricky could recognize the pain and difficulty Jimmy was enduring.

When the crowd entered the fellowship hall for the reception, Jimmy was seated in the receiving line, while Jenny stood at his side. Ricky could tell the long service and subsequent lengthy photography session had taken its toll on Jimmy. But Jimmy maintained a huge smile as he laughed and cut up with everyone passing through the receiving line.

Jimmy's truck was properly adorned, with Oreos stuck to the windows and body as well as two long strings of Budweiser and Busch beer cans tied to the rear bumper. A crowd tossed handfuls of rice as Jimmy and Jenny scampered to the truck for their honeymoon trip to Panama City Beach.

Saturday, January 6, 2001

Allen Madding

{ 27 }

Ricky was wiping down the rescue squad at the Haggard City Fire Department with a chamois skin to prevent water spots after washing the truck at the end of his shift when his cell phone vibrated. After Jimmy's wreck, Ricky had volunteered with the Whitiker County Fire Department while still working on the family farm. He then went to school to get his EMT certification. No one that knew him was surprised when he excelled at vehicle extrication and graduated at the top of his EMT class. Upon graduation, he was offered positions with several neighboring county ambulance services, but he eventually took a full-time job with the city fire department, where he quickly rose through the ranks.

Ricky tossed the chamois skin on the edge of a nearby chair and answered the phone. He recognized the voice on the other end to be Jenny.

"Ricky, we're at the hospital with Jimmy," she started.

He grimaced as she gave him the news. Jimmy had developed a high fever and had been experiencing significant pain in his hip and thigh. She had taken him in to see his orthopedic surgeon, who had admitted him to the hospital. Jimmy had developed a serious infection, and the doctors were trying to treat it as aggressively as possible.

Ricky hung up and immediately dialed Mary.

"Hey, babe. Jimmy has been hospitalized with a fever and an infection. I am going to run up to the hospital before I come home. You and the kids go ahead and eat dinner without me. I'll warm something up when I get home."

Mary understood the gravity of the situation. "OK, cowboy," she said. "Drive careful, and we'll be praying for him."

Ricky briefly spoke to the crew coming on shift and headed to the hospital in his pickup.

When he arrived at the hospital, he found Jenny reading a book and two kids playing a card game in the surgery waiting area.

"What's the word?" he asked as he approached them.

Jenny looked up, revealing red, puffy eyes. "He was complaining of pain in his hip, but in his typical stubbornness wouldn't let me carry him to the doctor until he developed a fever. I didn't argue with him at that point. Me and the kids loaded him up in the minivan and brought him. They've taken him into surgery to see if it's something to do with where they rebuilt his hip years ago."

Ricky nodded. "You kids had anything to eat?"

Jimmy's son and daughter looked up and shook their heads no.

"Ya'll hungry?" he asked.

"Yes, sir," the little boy answered.

He looked up at Jenny. "I'm gonna take these two down the street to McDonDon's and get them both a Happy Meal. You want anything?"

She shook her head no.

"You sure?" he asked. "I can pick up something from somewhere better for you."

"Nah," she said. "I can't eat. I'll grab a cup of coffee in a bit."

"Alright," Ricky replied. "Let's roll, you two."

When Ricky returned with the kids an hour or so later, he found Jenny nursing a Styrofoam cup of coffee and staring at a TV.

"Any word?" he asked.

Jenny nodded. "He's in recovery. They've inserted a drain in his hip and now we wait."

Ricky hung out with Jenny and the kids as they waited for Jimmy to get a hospital room. After another hour, a nurse rolled a bed down the adjoining hall—Jimmy. The patient rolled his head toward the group when they rolled him into the room.

They quietly followed him in. Jenny gave him a kiss, and he squeezed the hands of both children at his bedside. Jimmy looked pale, his hair thinning a bit, but still sported a beard, now beginning to gray, that covered his neck. He looked over at Ricky standing near the doorway.

"Well, look what the dog drug in and the cat wouldn't cover up," he said.

Ricky grinned. "Hell of a way to get a day off from the parts counter, ain't it?"

Jimmy chuckled groggily. "That place is gonna go to hell if I don't get back there shortly." He grimaced from pain and then continued. "Them young kids don't know crap from shoe polish. They have to go to the computer for anything any customer needs."

Ricky laughed. "Yeah, if you need wiper blades, they wanna know if it has an automatic transmission or not."

Jimmy shook his head. "Exactly! One of 'em aggravated me the other day, so I told him a customer needed a fuel pump for a Ford 8N tractor." He paused again for a wave of pain. "Lil bastard spent two hours researching, trying to figure that one out, before I finally told him an 8N was gravity fed and didn't have a fuel pump." He paused again and drew a slow breath. "How's your crew doing?"

"They're fine. The kids think we need a swimming pool. I am trying to get them to understand we're running a farm, and I am working at the fire department. We don't exactly have the budget for a pool."

Jimmy nodded. "Kids! We were fine swimming in your family's pond."

"Yeah," Ricky replied. "Times have changed, I guess."

"You're right about that," Jimmy said. "We're trying to arrange things to enroll these two in the new charter school. Kids ain't cheap."

"Well, bud, I think I prolly should scoot and check on my two before they get put to bed," Ricky said.

"Alright, buddy," Jimmy said, holding out his hand.

Ricky grabbed his hand and gave it a firm handshake.

"Try to do what they tell you and get feeling better," Ricky said. "If y'all need anything, just holler."

"Will do," Jimmy replied.

"Thanks for coming," Jenny said, and gave Ricky a hug before he walked out of the room. She looked tired and troubled, with dark lines under her eyes. As he made his way home, Ricky felt an overwhelming heaviness in his stomach concerning Jimmy's condition.

***

Four nights later, Ricky woke to his phone ringing. When he answered, he could hear Jenny crying.

"He's gone, Ricky," she stammered. "He just passed away."

Ricky struggled to compose himself and find words.

"I'm so sorry, Jenny," he finally heard himself say.

"I'll call you when we get plans together," she said before hanging up.

Ricky sat up in the bed, staring into the darkness.

***

The morning of Jimmy's funeral, Ricky found himself looking at Buck as the two of them and Jimmy's brother and three other pallbearers set in a small room off of the sanctuary listening to the funeral director give them instructions. He hadn't spoken to Buck since the night of the wreck. In fact, he had intentionally avoided him and ignored him any time they had crossed paths over the last nineteen years. Buck looked disheveled with his thinning hair hanging in his eyes, his skin wrinkled, dull, and gray, and his nose large and purple.

Ricky sat through the entire service wearing his dark sunglasses. He didn't hear a word spoken during the service, lost in his thoughts and memories. Once they loaded the casket into the hearse, he joined Mary and his kids at their SUV to follow the procession to the graveyard. After the graveside service was completed, Ricky hugged Jenny and her kids.

He was walking a few steps behind his family, headed for their SUV, when he spotted Buck out the corner of his eye, standing alone a few steps away. Ricky thought he looked smug and indifferent. Ricky felt the muscles tighten in his right arm and his face turn red. Without a word, he turned toward Buck and sped up his pace. When he reached Buck, his right fist shot out and connected squarely with the middle of Buck's face. The force of the punch folded Buck's knees, and he fell to the ground like a bag of potatoes. Before Buck could mount any kind of defense, Ricky leapt on top of him, pinning his shoulders to the ground with his knees, and landed two more punches to his face before four men drug him off.

"You killed him, you bastard!" Ricky shouted as he struggled to free himself from the grip of the four men. "You killed him. It just took him nineteen years to die from it, but you killed him, you worthless piece of crap."

Ricky shoved the men off of him, brushed off his clothes, and walked back to his startled family at their SUV. He looked up at Mary's disappointed stare and the shock in the face of his two kids.

"I'm sorry y'all had to see that," Ricky said, his guilt for embarrassing his family conflicting with his satisfaction in delivering overdue justice. "But he's had that coming for nineteen years and today was the day."

{ 28 }

S everal months after the funeral, Ricky and Mary were sitting at the kitchen table looking at the day's mail. Mary handed Ricky a card.

"I think you're going to find this a bit odd," she said.

"Oh?" Ricky responded, taking the card and flipping it open. He shook his head in disbelief. "We knew Jimmy's little brother had divorced his wife, and I'd heard he was seeing Jenny. But do they really think we'd go to their wedding? This is just messed up. It's crazy!"

Mary nodded in agreement.

"I'm at a loss," Ricky said as he drew a sip of coffee. He crumpled the invitation in his fist and tossed it at the trash can a few feet away.

"Everyone deals with their pain in different ways," Mary noted quietly.

"I guess so," Ricky replied. "Buck's suicide was his method and this is Jenny's." His words trailed off as he felt a knot in his stomach and he recalled his last words with his former friend at Jimmy's funeral.

Ricky's melancholy was interrupted when he heard Mary gasp. He looked up to see her move her hands to her belly.

"Your son is rambunctious today!" she said with a grin. "Have you thought of any boys' names?"

"I'd like to name him James Lowe Mann in honor of Jimmy, if that's alright with you," he quietly answered as his eyes began to tear up.

"I think that would be a wonderful tribute," Mary said as she leaned over, wiped a tear from his cheek, and softly kissed him.

Other Books
by Allen Madding

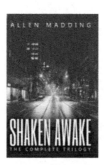

Shaken Awake: The Complete Trilogy
by Allen Madding

A dreadful chill ravages the city and a homeless man is found
frozen to death on the church steps...

The city of Atlanta had weathered a thousand wet and chilly
days in winter with occasional snowfall... but never one like this.
A snowfall that begins in the noon turns into a vicious ice storm
by evening, obliterating everything in its way. People are stuck
into the whiteout, and trying to look for a way out.

Now, as the Peachtree Church opens its door to those out in
cold, the church members come face to face with a stark reality.
As uncomfortable truths make themselves known, this storm
will prove be to an eye opener for many.

Enlightening and compelling, Shaken Awake brings to surface a
truth we either ignore or just don't know. With richly textured
characters, haunted by the memories of their past, Shaken
Awake is both a deeply engrossing novel and a thought-
provoking piece of social commentary.

Lendercide
by Allen Madding

In her work as a loan processor at Sunshine City Bank in Saint Petersburg, Colleen Smithwick has always found it hard to cope with the increasing pressures of work–suffering myopic and tyrannical loan officers while grinding through unreasonable deadlines. She plays the part of a committed wife well, but a restlessness weighs heavy on her mind. When murders of two high-officials rock the bank, Colleen becomes enamored with the lead detective investigating the case.

It's Detective Gary Black's job to see the risk in every situation, but he is unaware of the danger surrounding his own life. Since the time he first met Colleen, he has felt a strange attraction for her, the attraction that leads him into a world of dark secrets, throwing him into the path of a psychopathic killer. He must do whatever it takes to solve the case. That is, if he can stay ahead in the game.

Allen Madding

<u>Volunteer Management 101:</u>
<u>How to Recruit and Retain Volunteers</u>
by Allen Madding and Dan King

An employee needs the paycheck to pay the rent, the mortgage, the car payment, student debt, the credit card bill, the utilities, and a host of other bills. Volunteers, on the other hand are not motivated by a paycheck to stick it out when the manger is chewing someone out or things get uncomfortable.

The volunteer is simply motivated by making a difference and being a part of the organization. Their commitment hinges on how vested they are with the vision and purpose of the organization. When it gets to be too much of a hassle to serve, when they feel unappreciated, or when they feel the commitment is too demanding, they will walk away – usually without any warning or explanation.

With several decades of experience between them, Madding and King share insights on how to manage these valuable resources in your organization.

ABOUT THE AUTHOR

Allen Madding is a follower of the way, author, traveler, Atlanta Braves and Dallas Cowboys fan, and an information technology professional who lives in Thomasville, Georgia. He grew up in rural South Georgia where he developed a love for hunting, fishing, putting peanuts in a Coca-Cola, and racing cars. He raced short track stock cars for nine years and has written for Speedway Media and Insider Racing News. He is a retired volunteer firefighter/NREMT-I and fancies himself as a storyteller and a guitar strummer.

He is always up for a road trip and a hot cup of truck stop coffee. He feels at home in wide open spaces, hiking in the woods, walking on the beach listening to the ocean's tide, watching the sunset over a cypress lined pond, and relishes the smell of honeysuckle and the sound of the wind through the pines.

He loves a medium rare steak, cheeseburgers, blackberry cobbler, bourbon and Coke, boiled peanuts from a roadside stand, and a hotdog and beer at a baseball game while heckling the opposing team and keeping the umpire honest. He roots for the underdog and has learned how to say "I'm sorry". He believes that Dale Earnhardt was the greatest driver to ever compete in NASCAR, that Chevrolet is the heartbeat of America, and that Ford is a four letter word.

He says "Yes, Sir" and "No Ma'am" and prays before a meal. He believes that scars are the original tattoos and has a collection of both that remind him where he has been and help to keep him headed in the right direction.

Summer of '82

Made in the USA
Columbia, SC
11 April 2022